# RETURN TO THE LOST LEVEL

BRIAN KEENE

ISBN 978-1-937009-63-2 (TPB)

Apex Publications, LLC
PO Box 24323
Lexington, KY 40524

Also available as a DRM-free eBook.

Visit us at www.apexbookcompany.com.

*For Joe and Karen Lansdale*

# [ 1 ]
# NOTES FROM THE DESERT

My name is Aaron Pace, and I'm writing this by hand in an accounting ledger that I found in an office building in the middle of the desert. The office building is old but new. By that, I mean it's an old building, or at least it looks old. The architectural design suggests it was built in the Seventies or Eighties, maybe, although I suppose that depends on *where* it was originally constructed, rather than *when*.

Regardless of where the building came from, it's old. The concrete walls are cracked and fissured, revealing the steel support beams and rebar deep inside them, and much of the building's interior drywall is pockmarked with holes. Entire sections of the drop ceiling have collapsed, and most of the windows are broken. There's an elevator shaft and a stairwell, but both are unusable and blocked with piles of debris. I don't know how many floors this building originally had, but now there are only two. Everything above the second story has been sheared off. I don't know if that happened before the building came here or after its arrival. Sand has filled much of the first floor and is creeping through the broken windows on the second floor, as well. I imagine in a short time, the desert will swallow this building up whole, and it will sink beneath the dunes, lost for all time like everything else in this place.

When I say the building is also new, I'm referring to its location here in the desert. The building itself might be old, but its presence here is a relatively new thing. I've been through this area before. Twice, in fact. Once by myself and another time with 9, a robotic companion with whom I travelled for quite a while. The office building wasn't here on either of those visits, which means it's a more recent arrival to the Lost Level.

That's what this dimension is called. If you've stumbled across the other journal I left behind (in the back of a school bus), then you already know that. If not—if you're new here—then perhaps a brief explanation is in order. I'll have to keep it short, though, because I could only find a few of these accounting ledgers that were suitable for my purposes.

I came to the Lost Level by accident, via something called the Labyrinth, which is best described as an interdimensional pathway of energy running through space and time. The Labyrinth touches and connects everything in our universe. Since all the planets, stars, and galaxies are connected together by the Labyrinth, madmen, magi, occultists, and other seekers can travel from planet to planet and star system to star system. But they can also travel to other dimensions and alternate realities. You see, just as there are different planets in the universe, there are also different versions of those planets. These other-dimensional realities are often referred to as "levels." The Labyrinth allows travel to and from these levels. Imagine an Earth where the Germans won World War II, or where China landed on the moon in the year 2002, or a version of Mars where, instead of arid, frigid desolation, one might find temperate jungles teeming with intelligent alien life. All of these exist, and all of them are accessible, if you know which doorway in the Labyrinth to open.

But there is one level that is different than all of these—a dimensional reality that exists apart from all the others, a place where the flotsam and jetsam of space and time occasionally wash up from across the shores of the multiverse. It is a place where one can encounter creatures and beings and objects from, quite literally, anywhere in the multiverse, and from any *time* in the multiverse, as well. That place is called the Lost Level, and if you are reading this, then you are in it, and you are screwed.

That's the first thing you should know.

The second thing you should know is that there's no escape from the Lost Level. There is no going home. No going back. The Labyrinth leads into this place, but there is no exit, except in death—and even then, scholars are divided. Some say souls and spirits can escape the Lost Level. Others say those energies remain trapped here for all time, just like everything else. I don't know who is right and who is wrong. Regardless, I can say with some authority that Jim Morrison was right when he said that no one gets out of here alive. On my world, there was a song by the Eagles that I think sums it up aptly—*you can check out anytime you like, but you can never leave.*

As I said before, I came to this place by accident. I had been using an occult ritual to explore alternate realities for some time, and sadly, I'd grown careless and cocky about it. Ultimately, that led to my being trapped here. One moment I was at home in Wisconsin, and the next, I was stranded here in the Lost Level with only the clothes on my back and the contents of my pockets. Full of despair and fear, I did my best to survive.

Eventually, I made friends with two other inhabitants. The first was Bloop, a strange, blue-furred cross between a cat and an ape who was as brave and agile and loyal a companion as one could ever hope to have. The other was Kasheena, the warrior princess of a local tribe, a ferocious and valiant fighter whose wits, cunning, and skill with a sword were matched only by her beauty. I first encountered Bloop and Kasheena when they were captives of the Anunnaki—a race of intelligent, bipedal snake men who also inhabit this place. The Anunnaki communicate via telekinesis, and they are ruthless, loathsome foes—a blight on every other individual stuck here. I am not ashamed to admit that I hate them with a xenophobic passion.

After I'd helped free Bloop and Kasheena from their bondage, we journeyed to Kasheena's village. It was a long trip, made longer by the fact that it is nearly impossible to mark the passage of time here in the Lost Level. That is because the sun never sets here. Indeed, it doesn't move at all. It simply hangs in the sky, hovering perpetually at high noon. It provides light and illumination, the way all suns do, but it is motionless. Judging by the amount of gray in my hair and the wrinkles on my face, I have been in the Lost Level for many years now, but in all that time, I have yet to unravel the mystery of the sun. I have suspicions regarding it—suspicions based on observations and things I've learned since my arrival. I don't think it's really a sun. I think it's an artificial construct. But to fully explain my thoughts surrounding its true origins and purpose, I could fill another of these accounting ledgers, and as I've said before, I don't have the time or the room to do that right now. Instead, I want to recount an earlier tale, from long ago, when the jungles and forests and deserts and caverns of this place were still a mystery to me.

On the way to Kasheena's village, we encountered other hazards and dangers—dinosaurs, giant robots, killer grass, and all other manner of deadly flora and fauna, including Grey aliens. Like the Anunnaki, the Greys have an established presence here in the Lost Level, although encounters with them are extremely rare. I've learned some things about them, just as I have the sun, but again, I don't have the space here to recount it all right now. Suffice to say, the Greys don't interact with the Lost Level's other living beings very often, and when they do, they always have an ulterior motive.

Kasheena saved my life numerous times during that journey. Indeed, most of the survival skills I've learned here came from her. Eventually, we reached her people, but at a terrible cost. Bloop was killed in the dark by a giant, monstrous slug while Kasheena and I slept just a few feet away from him. By the time we became aware of the danger, it was too late to save him. Indeed, we barely escaped with our own lives. We avenged our companion, killing the slug and others like it, but Bloop's horrific fate haunts me to this day. I mourned him for a long time.

I mourn him still.

I settled in among Kasheena's people, and made a life for myself in the village, growing close to her father, and to Shameal, the tribe's wise-man. In time, I no longer missed my home. Instead, the Lost Level became my home, and Kasheena's people became my family. Back in Wisconsin, I had merely been content. Here, in the Lost Level, living in Kasheena's village, I was happy.

Months after Bloop's death, I led a group of tribe members to the crashed wreckage of a Nazi flying saucer. The craft was leaking radioactive material, and our intent was to bury the wreckage to safeguard the rest of the Lost Level. Fifteen men and women accompanied me on that journey, including Shameal, who was very interested in seeing the technology for himself. We worked for what must have been several days, based on the number of sleeps we had, and constructed a large earthen mound over the crash site.

Satisfied that nothing or no one would stumble upon the radioactive hazard unawares again, we returned to the village only to find it in still-smoking ruins. Our people lay scattered, dead or dying, alongside the corpses of an equal number of Anunnaki. We learned from one of the injured that a massive force of snake-men had attacked the village while we were gone. They'd captured those they could restrain and slaughtered those they couldn't. Kasheena's father was among those who had died defending the community. The Anunnaki had been especially cruel with him, and we never did find all of his body. Many others were mutilated in the same way. And though the villagers had put up a fierce fight, in the end, they were overwhelmed by sheer numbers. Over seventy of our friends and family had been taken, including Kasheena.

I set out within a few hours, determined to track the Anunnaki. I was armed with a steel sword, my .45 revolver (made by a manufacturer that had never existed on my world), a leather sling, a dagger, and a rusty box cutter, as well as my fourteen remaining bullets for the revolver, a small pouch of round stones that served as sling ammunition, and two twelve gauge shotgun shells for which I had no corresponding weapon. I figured the latter might come in handy should I need a quick source of gunpowder—or on the off chance I came across a twelve-gauge shotgun among the other debris constantly being transported to the Lost Level.

Despite his protests, I made Shameal remain behind to guide and lead what was left of the tribe, and tend to the injured. But I did not go alone. I was accompanied by a group of two dozen men and women. Some of them were warriors. Others had little or no experience with weapons or fighting but longed for revenge.

What follows here in these accounting ledgers is the story of that journey, one from which most of us didn't return. It led us into the very heart of the Anunnaki's city, where we found permanent darkness amidst the eternal sunlight.

## [ 2 ]
## BELOW AND ABOVE

The Anunnaki were easy enough to track. The group that attacked the village had been large, and although our people cut their numbers significantly during the assault, there were still dozens left alive—enough of them to forcefully march our captive tribe members under guard at a hurried pace. We estimated that in addition to the seventy of our loved ones held in bondage, there were approximately thirty or so snake men left alive. A force that size left signs of its passage, whether it wanted to or not.

The village's boundaries encompassed the surrounding plains and a small but dense forest at their center. Our village lay amidst that forest. I led the way as we followed our foes out onto those plains, wondering as I did just how the Anunnaki—especially such a large group of them—had managed to surprise our fellow tribesmen. There were always guards posted at the edges of our domain, scanning the horizons for any sign of approaching danger. The plains offered little protection or concealment for an approaching foe. They were a flat, rocky expanse about the length of five football fields populated only by short, scrubby weeds and a few groves of thin, stunted trees. How was it that an invading army had made it across that wide-open space and into the forest, attacking the village before an alarm was raised?

We hurried along, following the ruts and gouges their passage had left in the earth. Beyond the plains was an immense stretch of grassland, and the trail led toward it. We passed by the end of the tribe's territory, marked by the Temple of the Slug. The immense structure towered starkly against the flat terrain. It stood three stories high and was shaded by several tall, broad trees unlike the other squat vegetation on the plains. Even though I knew that it no longer held any danger, I shuddered as we passed by the shadow of the temple's domed roof. It was inside that ominous structure where Bloop had met his end, and though we had since slain all of the foul creatures who had dwelled there (thus the onus for the temple's name), seeing it now filled me with a deep sense of loathing and despair. I remembered all too well how he had died, crushed and drained beneath the bulk of a monstrous white slug. I remembered, too, how we had eventually slaughtered all of the giant slugs with weapons dipped in salt. These days, the tribe used the temple's secure walls to store grain and vegetables and other food, as well as utilizing it as a place of shelter during emergencies like the powerful thunderstorms that occasionally passed through the region. But neither Kasheena nor I had set foot past the stone pillars marking its entrance since killing the slugs, nor would we again. It was just too painful to do so.

Although I tried hard to hide them, some of the others must have picked up on my maudlin thoughts. I had been in the lead of our party, but now two of my companions, Karenk and Tolia, caught up to me, hurrying along at my side. Karenk had initially been a rival of mine when I'd first come to live among Kasheena's people. He'd been one of many potential suitors hoping to court Kasheena, but unlike some of the others, he had graciously stepped aside when she made her interest in me clear. Since then, he and I had formed an easygoing acquaintanceship, if not an outright friendship. Tolia was a friend of Kasheena's. The two had known each other almost since birth. I liked her very much. She was always smiling and able to find laughter in anything. But her mirth seemed gone now. I glanced back behind us, and saw no sign of her mate, Heresh, or their son, Apotic. Immediately, I feared the worst.

"Aaron." Tolia's expression was grim. Her forehead shined with sweat and dirt.

"Tolia." I nodded in greeting. "Where are Heresh and Apotic?"

"Heresh is dead. Apotic was taken."

My fears confirmed, I shook my head sadly. "I'm so sorry, Tolia."

"Do not be sorry for me, Aaron. Heresh lived long enough for me to say goodbye to him."

"How did he ...?"

"They hacked his legs off as they captured our son. He crawled after them until he grew weak from blood loss. I found him on the ground, and we had a chance to bid each other farewell. So, there is that. And Apotic will not be harmed during their journey. We know from previous kidnappings that the Anunnaki wish for their captives to remain alive until they reach their final destination."

"Well, I'm still sorry, Tolia."

"Save your pity for the snake men."

"No chance of that," I said. "The only thing I have for them is pain."

Tolia nodded, staring straight ahead. A swarm of gnats, as if sensing her mood, darted out of her way as she strode on.

"Your son will be fine," Karenk told her. "Remember that Kasheena is also a captive. No matter what kind of bondage the

Anunnaki have them in, she will not let harm befall Apotic. She would die first."

"You're right about that." I searched my memory, trying to remember if Karenk had loved ones that might be among the captives or slain. I hated the fact that I didn't know, for sure. Karenk was a fellow tribesman. I should have known if he had family or not. "Karenk—did you ... did you have any ...?"

"My parents are with the dead now, Aaron. I tell myself that it is better this way ... that being marched in captivity would have been harder on them, but ..."

His voice trailed off. Shrugging, he looked away from us, stifling a sob.

"I'm sorry, Karenk."

"Thank you, Aaron. But as you said to Tolia, I will help you deal pain to our enemies. I am saving it up inside myself. There is much pain to be given to them."

He was armed with a thick, crudely-hewn iron sword, and wore a stainless-steel kitchen knife in a sheath around his waist. The sheath was made from the skin of a Slukick, a squirrel-like rodent common here in the Lost Level. Tolia carried a bow and a quiver of arrows. I'd been on hunts with her and knew that she was a deadly markswoman. Both of them wore animal skins, in the fashion of the tribe—boots to protect their feet and enough covering to protect their most sensitive and vulnerable regions without compounding the heat of the day (modesty was not common amongst the tribe). In Karenk's case, his attire was fashioned from a saber-tooth tiger, while Tolia's was fashioned from the fur of a strange animal none of us had ever seen before. I had been there when she killed it. It resembled a cheetah, but the fur was sleeker and water repellant, and the beast had sported two antennae behind its ears.

Eventually, we reached the end of the plains and the start of the grasslands. From here, the trail was even easier to follow. A large swath of grass had been flattened, marking the passage of the Anunnaki and their prisoners. I called a brief halt, allowing everyone to catch their breath and quench their thirst, while I stared out at the swaying grass. The vegetation was taller than my head, and thus, it was impossible to see how far ahead our quarry actually were. But I knew which way they were going. Because there is no north here in the Lost Level, and because the sun never sets, directions like east or west are meaningless. As a result, denizens of this place navigate in different ways. The Anunnaki were marching the captives toward a distant mountain peak. I had never been there, nor had any of the others in our group. Between that mountain and our present location were the grasslands, and then a dense section of forested jungle, the outskirts of which could be seen far in the distance, lost in the shimmering heat haze.

"Karenk," I called, "can you give me a hand?"

He frowned in confusion, and glanced down at his palms, turning them over as if considering which appendage to chop off. I grinned. This was not the first time my figures of speech had caused trouble amongst the tribe.

"I am not sure I understand, Aaron. Are you asking me to—?"

"Don't worry." I laughed. "I just want to sit on your shoulders so I can get a better view across the plains. It's so flat here and you're the tallest among us."

Karenk's expression was one of clear relief. Smiling, he hurried over to me.

"I thought you wished me to cut off a hand for some ritual," he explained. "I would follow you anywhere, but I am afraid that would have been too much to ask."

"Nope, you can keep your hands and feet. I just need a boost."

He knelt on one knee and cupped his hands together. I clambered up onto his shoulders. Grunting, Karenk rose to his full height. Despite his strength, I felt him trembling beneath me, and resolved to survey the region as quick as possible. I suspected we had a long trek ahead of us yet, and I needed him to reserve his stamina.

The ever-present, never-setting sun beat down on us. Shielding my eyes with my hands, I scanned the plains, studying the terrain between us and the forest. Far ahead, at the base of the outer tree line, I spotted a large group of moving dots fading in and out of the shimmering heat haze.

"Okay." I patted Karenk's shoulder. "That's good. I see them. You can put me down now."

After I was back on the ground, Tolia and the rest of our fellow pursuers gathered around me. I knelt among them and pulled my dagger. Then, I quickly cleared away a patch of grass and began to draw in the dirt with the tip of my blade.

"We are here, and the snake men are here, along with their captives. They were just entering the tree line when I saw them, which means they're making much better time than we had anticipated."

"Which also means they are pressing their captives much harder than we thought they would," Tolia pointed out.

I nodded. "But that's actually a good thing."

"How is it a good thing if our loved ones die from exertion before we rescue them?" Tolia asked.

"Because it means they will be dead before they reach their final destination," another man, Apok, said.

Dismayed murmurs ran through the crowd.

Annoyed with Apok, I raised my voice to get their attention once again. "It also means that they'll have to stop soon and rest. We know they want to keep the captives alive. Yes, they may be running them hard now, but they won't run them to the point of death. My guess is they want our people so exhausted that they'll be too tired to even consider escaping. All we have to do is keep our pace, and not stop. When they rest—and they will rest, sooner or later—we'll close the distance. So, before we start off again, are there any questions?"

Apok pushed his way forward through the crowd. "Yes, I have a question."

"Go ahead."

"Why are you in charge? Why do you lead us?"

"Excuse me?"

"I remember when you first came to us, not far from the spot we stand at now, nearly dead, swooning, raving like a madman, and weeping for that beast you called a friend."

I rose slowly, sheathing my dagger. My hand stole to the hilt of my sword.

"All of this is true," I admitted, staring him in the eye. "But speak of my friend again like that and I will spread your guts out on the ground right here. Bloop fought hard to return Kasheena to all of you. He was a warrior, not a beast."

Apok's eyes darted to the hilt of my blade, then back up to mine. "And yet now the princess is gone again, and her father is slain. It seems to me you have failed at protecting them both. Perhaps it would be better if someone born among our tribe were to lead."

"Aaron Pace has proven his loyalty and his bravery to us time and time again," Tolia said. "You're a man of machinations, Apok. He is a man of honor."

"Aye," Karenk agreed. "I will follow him."

"Enough," I said, removing my hand from my sword. "I am going after our loved ones. Those of you who wish to follow me—I welcome your courage. Those of you who do not wish to follow me are still welcome to journey alongside us. We're all heading in the same direction, and we all want the same thing. We can argue about who belongs and who is fit to lead after we've rescued our people and killed every last Anunnaki."

We hurried on, following the path through the grasslands. I stayed out front, with Tolia and Karenk at my side. I wondered if Apok was behind me, looking for a place to thrust a knife in my back. I had never paid much attention to him during my time living with the tribe. In truth, I'd never cared to. He was conniving and duplicitous, and many of our warriors held him in contempt. And yet, he had grown up with Kasheena's father, who held his friendship in some regard. It was clear to me now, if not to the others, that Apok intended to make the most of the uncertainty of the tribe's current situation and set himself up as leader. But why, then, had he volunteered to accompany us on this rescue mission? I couldn't make sense of it, and decided not to dwell on it again until after we had rescued the others.

Nothing else moved around us, save for the breeze, rustling through the grass. The sky was empty of birds, the ground devoid of animals or insects. The last time I had come this way, it had been with Kasheena and Bloop. We had encountered an octophant—an elephantine creature with many tentacle-like trunks. The creature had been giving birth. The moment had been one of my favorites from this place, and even now, writing about it years later, the memory makes me smile. But it had also been ruined when a group of Anunnaki had attacked us just moments after the beast gave birth. I thought of that then, running across the plains—of how the snake-men ruined everything, of the blight they were on this land, this dimension, and I swore that I would not stop until I had exterminated each and every one of them. Like every other living thing within the Lost Level, the Anunnaki had come here from elsewhere, but unlike the other denizens of this level, they upset the natural balance of the place.

My time in this dimension had changed me, stripping away the veneer of civilization. Before, I would have viewed genocide as abhorrent. Now, I viewed it as our only solution. In order for us to survive, the Anunnaki had to be obliterated. None of them could be left alive.

We pushed on, determined. The sun beat down upon us, and sweat stung my eyes. I don't know how long we ran, but the forest seemed to draw no closer. The terrain stayed the same, rising and falling slightly on occasion, but mostly remaining flat. We stuck to the path, following the swath of crushed grass.

And then, the ground began to shake and soil exploded. There was a great upheaval in the midst of our ranks. I heard several of our number cry out in fear. Those of us in the front of the vanguard spun around to look behind us. Those in the rear faltered, falling back in terror. Thrusting from the earth was a giant, segmented worm. Our passage must have disturbed it. The creature was big enough that it had swallowed one of the tribesmen. Only his feet were visible, wriggling in the beast's gaping maw. The beast swayed back and forth, swallowing its prey whole, looming over the rest of us, as if choosing which one to eat next. I saw no eyes or visible sensory organs. Just that terrible, toothless mouth. Dirt clung to the worm's slimy, gray and pink skin. Its hide looked rubbery, but thick, and was composed of concentric rings, each about five feet wide. The thing's form reminded me of pictures I'd once seen in an occult tome back on Earth—an artist's depiction of the spawn of Behemoth, an ancient, monstrous, worm-like deity who originated from a universe that existed before our own. I estimated that roughly ten feet of the monster protruded from the ground, and could only imagine how much of it still lurked beneath our feet.

Panicked, a few of the tribe scattered, fleeing into the high grass on both sides of the path. Apok was among them. I spotted him slinking and ducking, his eyes and mouth wide with terror, so shocked that he hadn't even drawn his weapon.

The same could not be said of Tolia or Karenk. Both of them met our loathsome foe head-on, even as its massive head darted downward, snatching up another of our party. This time the victim was a woman, a huntress named Parrell. She was armed with a bow, but before she could notch an arrow, the worm fell upon her, sucking her into its maw with a disgusting slurping noise. I shuddered at the sound and brandished my sword. Karenk charged ahead, slashing at the monster near ground level. The rubbery flesh parted like blubber beneath his blade, but instead of blood, a noxious, watery, clear fluid gushed from the wound. Thrashing, the worm spat out Parrell and focused on Karenk. I ran to help him, but before I could, two arrows whizzed past me, striking the worm in its mid-section and head. A third missile zipped by. I glanced behind me and saw Tolia, already notching a fourth arrow. Her speed was amazing. Luckily for me, so was her aim.

Enraged, the worm quivered and swayed. Then, it tried to sink back down into its hole. Karenk and I struck it repeatedly with our swords, slashing and stabbing. Other tribe members rushed to our side and quickly joined the fray, attacking it with spears and clubs and other weapons. The beast shuddered and convulsed and reared up again. We fell back, out of its reach. Quivering, the worm collapsed onto the plain, with nearly a quarter of its length still sticking out of the ground.

"Everybody stay back," I ordered. "It might still have some fight left."

I prodded the monster experimentally with the tip of my sword. The worm twitched a few times, but then was still. More of that noxious fluid leaked from dozens of wounds, and smelling strongly of ammonia. The stench burned my nose, and my eyes watered.

"Have any of you ever seen one of these before?" I asked the group.

They all stared at me, shaking their heads or shrugging.

"Okay," I sighed. "I think it's blood might be toxic—poisonous. We should keep our distance from the carcass. And let's spread out a bit in case there are more of them. We'll still walk single file, but keep some distance between each other."

"For what reason?" asked one of the tribesmen.

"I suspect this thing was waiting beneath the ground. When it sensed us passing overhead, it attacked. If we keep spaced apart, it will give us better odds against another attack."

"We don't know that," Apok challenged. "Indeed, for all we know, you led us this way on purpose, Aaron Pace."

There was a grumbling of agreement among a few of the tribe members, but I was glad to hear louder dissent from the majority of the rescue party. Apok glared at me, grinning.

I met his stare, refusing to look away. "What are you implying, Apok?"

"What do we really know about you? Kasheena says she first encountered you while a prisoner of the Anunnaki. Those same Anunnaki have just raided our village. Perhaps you are in league with them. Perhaps you are a spy—a traitor to your own race. For all we know, you led us directly into this worm's path to slow down our pursuit. I say we—"

My .45 had cleared its holster and was in his face before I even realized I'd drawn it. Apok's malicious grin vanished as he stared down the barrel of the handgun. I poked his nose with it, watching his sweat bead on the metal.

"I warned you once, Apok."

He held his hands out at his sides, indicating surrender. His gaze flickered from the gun, and then back up to me. Slowly, his grin returned.

"Are you going to kill me, Aaron? Slay one of the very warriors helping in your effort to bring back our captured people? Perhaps this is simply another way of thinning our numbers?"

"This is a revolver, Apok. I don't expect you to know the difference, but unlike other handguns, revolvers don't have a safety. So the next sound you hear is going to be me pulling the trigger. You won't hear the blast. You'll be dead by then."

"Aaron," Tolia called, her tone urgent.

I glanced in her direction and saw her kneeling by the fallen archer Parrell, whom the worm had spit out during our assault. Then I quickly looked back to Apok.

"Is she alive?" I asked, not taking my eyes off my rival.

"She does not wake," Tolia reported, "but she breathes still. Her leg is broken."

"We don't have time for your shit," I told Apok. "Take Parrell back to the village."

"No," he replied. "I will stay and safeguard my people—from the snake men and from any other threats."

My grip tightened on the handle of the .45. "It wasn't a request, Apok."

He shrugged. "And yet, my answer remains the same, *outsider*."

The village tanner, a burly man named Oxsmith, stepped forward. "Enough of this. I will take Parrell back to the village. Then I will rejoin you."

I eyed him, hesitating.

"Do not let my girth fool you, outsider. I am faster than a thunderbird. Continue on, and I will find my way back before you have even reached the forest."

"Very well." Nodding, I lowered my weapon and stepped slowly backward. It was not lost on me that Oxsmith had mimicked Apok's slur—calling me an outsider. Before now, I had always been on friendly terms with the man. I wondered if he was even aware he'd done it.

Tolia tried collecting arrows from the worm's carcass, but recoiled from the ammonia-like stench pouring from its wounds. Instead, she picked up a few unbroken shafts that had missed their mark and fallen on the ground. She distributed these among the other archers in the group. Then she unstrung Parrell's bow and stored the spare string in her quiver.

I surveyed the rest of the crowd. I don't know if it was my imagination, but it seemed to me that more of them looked at me with suspicion or disdain than they had before. It wasn't an outright revolt—not yet. But if Apok continued to sow seeds of discontent, it could turn into one fairly quickly. The villagers were scared, leaderless, and angry. They wanted somebody—anybody—to blame, and since we'd yet to find any Anunnaki for them to vent their rage on, I was beginning to make a fine scapegoat, no matter how illogical it might be. It occurred to me then that these people were not so different than the people back on Earth. Sure, they loved and laughed just as we'd done back home, but they also harbored the same fears and prejudices. Sure, maybe here in the Lost Level, the apprehensiveness stemmed from the possibility of getting eaten by a dinosaur rather than dying of cancer or a terrorist bombing, but human fear was still human fear, and xenophobia knew no dimensional boundaries.

"There's a tree line ahead," I said to the assembled hunters. "The serpent men have taken our loved ones into it. And when I say our loved ones, I mean just that. *Our*. Most of you have welcomed me into your tribe many sleeps ago. If I am no longer welcome among you—if I am not considered to be one of you—we can discuss that, and who should lead you, later. Right now, we need to focus on the task at hand. Oxsmith is going to take Parrell back to the village. The rest of us are going to press ahead. We're going to stay spaced out, in case there are more worms, but we're also going to push hard. We can't afford any more delays. If they get too far into the forest, we'll have a hard time tracking them. Now, grab your gear and let's go. Are there any objections?"

About half of them voiced their affirmation. A few murmured negatively, but there was no large outcry or dissent. Satisfied, I holstered my pistol, drew my sword, and led us forward again, sweeping through the tall grass and following the trail. I glanced behind once to see Oxsmith bearing our fallen archer back toward the village, and caught sight of Apok slinking along at the rear of our procession.

We were delayed twice more before reaching the tree line. The first time was when a looming shadow fell over us. We hunkered down in the grass, hiding as a large pterodactyl soared far overhead. Luckily, the beast didn't spot us—or if it did, the thing decided we outnumbered it and wouldn't make for an easy meal. It flew on, disappearing toward the mountains. The second delay occurred when we came across one of our villagers—a young woman named Slurra, lying dead to one side of the path. She bore no obvious signs of fatality. No wounds or injuries. Nor were there any indications on the ground around her of what might have occurred. I saw no blood, or scores and slashes from weaponry. No signs of a fight or struggle of any kind.

"Perhaps she died from grief and despair," Karenk suggested quietly.

None of us argued with that hypothesis.

"She will be avenged," another villager promised.

"We should bury her," Apok said. "It is not right to leave her body here like this, where it can be eaten by scavengers."

I nodded. "I agree, but there is no time. Perhaps you could carry her back to the village, Apok? I'm sure her family would appreciate it."

He glared at me for a long moment, and then glanced around at the others.

"No, I will stay the course. As you said, there is no time. But we should cut the grass and cover her with it—and mark this spot, so we do not forget her upon our return."

I shrugged. "Very well."

Several villagers slashed at the grass with their swords and knives, cutting down a wide section of vegetation. Then they piled the clippings over Slurra's body, concealing it. Meanwhile, I cut a large X into the ground with the tip of my dagger.

"Satisfied?" I asked Apok.

He grunted.

"I'll take that as a yes."

The grass thinned before we reached the tree line, and it became increasingly difficult to conceal ourselves among the stunted blades. I brought us to a halt when we were about one hundred yards away. I had been to this spot before, and not that long ago, during an ill-fated hunting trip with Kasheena. Then, we had encountered a Chinese manufactured, tank-like probe of some kind, along with an angry mother triceratops and her litter of newborns. The dinosaur had destroyed the robot, so I had no fears of crossing paths with it again. What worried me now was how we could break cover and reach the forest without being seen.

We crouched there, gathered close together, and debated what to do next. Every time I voiced a strategy or plan, Apok would find fault with it, encouraging the others to do the same. I admit—I lost my temper with him again, and we ended up arguing.

That proved to be our undoing.

We learned later that the Anunnaki, perhaps spotting our pursuit across the plain, had left behind a group of archers, who had hidden themselves in the tops of the trees while the rest of their party continued on with their captives. We were unaware of these archers' presence until their arrows began to whistle down upon our clustered ranks, sprouting from throats and shoulders and backs.

Shouting, our forces panicked and scattered, scrambling in all directions to avoid the rain of missiles. More of our ranks were brought down as a second volley struck. I spotted Karenk with his sword drawn, glancing wildly about as if expecting the bowmen to rise up out of the grass. I was about to shout to him to get down when I tripped over a fallen tribe member and crashed to the ground, knocking the wind from me. Doing so saved my life, as another shaft buzzed through the air where I'd been standing just a second before.

As I struggled to regain both my breath and my footing, I saw Tolia duck down and notch an arrow. Then she sprang up and loosed the missile. Without waiting to see if the arrow found its mark, she darted to another spot, where she crouched back down and repeated the attack. She did this all across the field, avoiding enemy arrows while firing her own, but she was too far away. The reptilian bowmen had the advantage of higher ground, which helped their range. Our own archers couldn't compete with that. If we stayed where we were, caught out in the open, we'd be slaughtered. Our only choices were to retreat or charge. I thought of Kasheena, a captive of those cold-blooded, scaly bastards, and decided that retreating would be no better than standing here waiting to die.

Clambering to my feet, I drew my sword and held it high. "Listen up! All of you! Follow me!"

Then I charged across the field, running in a crisscross pattern to confuse the hidden archers. Karenk and others followed my lead, dashing toward the tree line from different angles, darting back and forth, and even doubling back, all to provide a more difficult target.

I glanced back only once and noticed that those who had followed my attack were—like myself—almost to the trees. With some dismay, I saw that those who hadn't were being struck down as they fled in panic. We had started this rescue mission with two dozen tribesmen, but those numbers were steadily dwindling.

Slipping into the shadow of the forest, I ducked down and paused, scanning the foliage for the enemy. The bushes to my right rustled as if some great beast were about to bear down on me, but then Karenk emerged, bloodied from where a passing arrow had carved a furrow in his bicep, but otherwise okay. We nodded at each other. He pointed at a nearby tree, indicating the archers' position. We crawled forward, creeping up to the trunk. Before we could climb, two more villagers joined us. I was surprised to see that Apok was one of them.

We huddled together beneath the tree. The leaves rustled far above us as the concealed archers bustled around.

"Where are the others?" I asked.

Karenk shook his head. "I do not know."

"Scattered," Apok whispered. "Or dead, thanks to your leadership."

"I saw two archers above us," Karenk said, hurriedly cutting off my response to Apok. "And two more in that tree yonder."

"They don't seem to be running out of arrows."

"No," Karenk agreed.

"We've got to put an end to this, and fast." I turned to the other villager—a teenage boy barely old enough to shave. Back on Earth, he'd have been learning how to drive, or falling in love for the first time, or maybe thinking about what college he wanted to go to. Not so here in the Lost Level. But that didn't make him any different than a teenager back home. He was just as young, and just as scared. "What's your name?"

When he answered, his voice quavered. "Martek."

"Okay, Martek. Can you climb?"

He nodded.

"Good." I looked him over. "You don't have a weapon."

"I had a spear, but I ... when the arrows started falling ... I dropped it."

I handed him my sword. He looked at it as if I were offering him a live snake.

"But ... but Aaron ...?"

"Take it," I whispered. "You know how to use one, right?"

He nodded again, and then took it nervously, holding it carefully.

"It's a good blade. I want that back when we're done."

I grinned, trying to set him at ease, but Martek only looked nauseous.

"Okay, Karenk—you and Martek take that tree over there. Apok, you and I will take the one above us."

"Me?" Apok blustered. "I don't think—"

"You wanted to be in charge. You wanted to lead. Now lead on, Apok."

Karenk chuckled softly. Apok glared at him and then at me.

"Very well. I am not afraid."

But he was. I knew that he was. It was apparent from the hesitation in his voice and the way he carried himself. It echoed in his sullen expression as, still chuckling, Karenk led Martek toward the other nearby tree. It showed in the color his ears turned as he began to climb. I won't lie—I enjoyed seeing his discomfort. Then, I heard our fellow tribe members shouting out on the plain, still under bombardment, and my attention returned to the task at hand. Making sure my revolver and dagger were both holstered safely, I sprang up into the tree and began to follow after him.

I don't know what world they came from, but these particular trees were unlike anything back on Earth. You have to be mindful of the vegetation here in the Lost Level. Just like everything else in this place—humans to dinosaurs to aliens to robots—the plant life comes from all across the universe and all of its myriad dimensions, and not all of the forms are pleasant or docile. A botanist could spend their entire life in this place and still not catalog them all. I've encountered things as innocuous as red pine trees or purple dandelions. But I've also seen grass that will cut you quicker and deeper than any razor, tree bark that acts like flypaper, vines that will creep into your camp and strangle you in your sleep, and even a walking, bipedal sort of oak that tosses exploding pinecones at anything it deems a threat.

The tree that Apok and I now climbed was similar to a palm tree in shape and texture, but it was much taller, and rather than fronds, it sported a bushy, leafy top supported by a vast network of thick limbs that spread out far around it—forming a natural platform of sorts. These limbs were only found at the top, however. The rest of the length of the trunk was bare, save for warty, knoblike protrusions of bark all along its length. They reminded me of the handholds on those artificially manufactured rock climbing walls back home, and we utilized them in much the same manner, carefully making our way upwards as stealthily as possible.

As we drew closer to the top, the tree limbs vibrated as the Anunnaki archers moved back and forth, picking their shots. The leaves rustled, but otherwise, the snake men made no sound. I saw a few more of our fellow tribe members sneaking through the forest below us, regrouping, but there was no sign of Tolia. I hoped she was okay. Across from us, I saw Karenk and Martek scaling the other tree. Then I turned my attention back to climbing.

Apok parted the branches and scurried up into the leaves. Carefully choosing my footing, I hurried after him, emerging into a broad, flat area, almost like a deck, formed by the expanding tree limbs. Two Anunnaki were perched atop these limbs, moving nimbly back and forth along thick, sturdy branches wider than Karenk's chest. Both opponents were armed with bows. A pile of arrows lay between them, balanced atop a thick blanket of leaves and supported by a cluster of thinner branches. Given how many they had already fired, I had to assume the heap had been bigger at one point. Both reptilians were clad in leather armor fashioned from human skin. It was not the first time I had seen the snake men wearing such garments, but the sight always sickened and angered me. Their backs were to us, giving us the element of surprise. Gritting my teeth, I pulled the revolver.

Lacking a ranged weapon, Apok drew his short sword and began to inch toward them, blocking my shot. Worse, his footsteps vibrated the tree limbs. I felt it through my own soles, and so did our opponents. Both whipped around quickly, forked tongues flicking at the air, reptilian eyes showing neither surprise or hate—their faces, like those of the rest of their kind—cold, expressionless masks. They raised their bows, arrows already notched to rain down upon our friends, and pointed them at us instead.

"Apok," I shouted, "drop!"

I half expected him to argue with me, to take exception with my command even in the face of death, but he didn't. Instead, my conniving companion ducked low, nearly losing his balance and slipping through the branches as a result. He scrambled for a handhold, struggling precariously. The first snake man loosed his arrow. It zipped through the air where Apok had been standing a mere second before. The second bowman swiveled toward me, but I shot him twice, aiming both rounds at his center mass. He made no sound as the bow slipped from his scaled hands. They never did. Even in death, the Anunnaki were silent. They communicated through telepathy. Maybe they screamed telepathically, as well. If so, I hoped at that moment that all of his kind heard him shriek as he crashed through the foliage and tumbled to the forest floor below.

The other archer reached for another arrow, but I shot him in the face. He stood there for a moment, swaying back and forth on the tree limb, before finally falling. He flopped about, blood splattering against the leaves, but managed to stay perched in the treetop, even after he lay still.

Panting for breath, Apok pulled himself back up onto the platform and shakily rose to his feet. His complexion was the color of cheesecloth, and his forehead shone with sweat. He glanced around at his feet and then bent over and retrieved his fallen short sword.

"You're lucky that didn't fall below."

He nodded.

I pointed at the fallen archer. "Check his corpse, Apok. Make sure he's dead."

Apok stared up at me and then glanced at the fallen Anunnaki with clear trepidation.

"The snake man's not moving. Surely he is dead."

Ignoring him, I flipped open the revolver's cylinder, and ejected the spent brass casings into my palm. I winced as the hot metal touched my flesh, but I didn't want to lose them. One of the keys to surviving in this place is to make do with what you have and never discard anything if you can at all help it. Everything can be repurposed and recycled. I've made knives from broken compact discs, fashioned fishing lures from bits of bone and electronic scraps, and turned an old rusty stop sign into a formidable shield. I've seen skulls turned into bowls and mugs, a canoe used as armor, and a hair dryer used as a flail. With that in mind, I dropped the empty brass into the leather pouch containing the ammunition for my sling and then blew on my blistered palm.

As a result, I didn't see the next arrow until after it had whistled by my head and buried itself in Apok's left eye.

Apok made a surprised, chortling sound, and swayed back and forth on his feet. A small dribble of blood trickled down his cheek. His left eye was gone, and half a feathered shaft jutted from the socket. He swayed back and forth on his feet and then toppled over face forward. The arrow snapped as he hit the branch.

I ducked low, scrambling for cover, and then spotted Tolia. She was crouched behind me, holding her bow. I gasped in surprise, realizing that it was she who had killed Apok.

"Tolia? When did you get here?"

"Just now." She nodded at the dead snake man. "I see you didn't leave any for me."

"I'm sure you'll have your fair share before we're done. Tolia —why did you ...?"

"Kill him?"

"Yeah."

She sauntered over to Apok's body. Kneeling, she flipped him over and checked his pulse. "Because he would have killed you the first chance he got. And probably Karenk and myself and anybody else who sided with you. Understand something, Aaron. The Anunnaki are not the only threat to our tribe right now. With her father dead, it falls to Kasheena to lead our people. She is his heir—his only heir. But she is among the captives. There are many who would take advantage of this situation to usurp control for themselves. Apok was only the loudest of them. There are others back in the village who will not make their intentions so obvious."

"Apok was a shithead," I agreed, "but he had his supporters, even among the warriors in our party. How are they going to react when they find out?"

She leaned over and grabbed an Anunnaki arrow from the pile. Then, she placed one foot on Apok's forehead, grasped her arrow with both hands, and slowly pulled, twisting and turning the shaft, taking care not to break it, until finally the missile was free. She tossed the bloody arrow down to the forest floor, and plunged the Anunnaki arrow into the wound. Then she looked up at me and smiled.

"When they find out he was shot by an Anunnaki? They will curse the snake men even more than they already do."

Before I could respond, Karenk called out to me, his voice echoing across the treetops.

"Hello, Aaron!"

I cupped my hand around my mouth. "All clear, Karenk. You?"

"We have bested our foes. Young Martek fought bravely."

"Excellent! We'll meet you guys down below."

Tolia and I made a quick search of the treetop, looking for any gear we might be able to scavenge, but found nothing. She refilled her quill from the pile of arrows, commenting on her distaste for the inferior shafts and arrowheads.

"What do we do with him?" I pointed at Apok's corpse.

She prodded his body with her toe and then pushed him off the limb. Branches snapped and rustled as he plummeted to the ground. Apok's corpse landed with a sound like a sack of wet potatoes. Tolia flashed me a look of mock innocence and batted her eyelashes.

"It's such a shame. He fell after he was shot. We could do nothing for him. It was too late."

Grinning, I shook my head. "You sure don't mess around, Tolia."

"Mess?" She frowned.

"Never mind. Just an expression from my world."

"I sometimes forget that you are not from our world, Aaron. I consider you one of us. You are a worthy addition to our tribe and Kasheena's bed."

"Thank you, Tolia. That might be the nicest thing anybody has said to me in quite some time."

"It is meant."

"Well, I appreciate it. You're pretty badass yourself."

"That is a compliment?" she asked.

I nodded. "It is."

"Then, thank you, Aaron. I will honor it."

We climbed back down to the forest floor, anxious to regroup with the rest of the party and continue our pursuit.

# [ 3 ]
# THE DETERMINED DOZEN

One by one, the survivors of the ambush gathered beneath the trees. Some were injured. Others had escaped the bombardment unscathed. When everyone from our party was finally accounted for, we discovered to our shock that only thirteen of us remained alive. Everyone else had been slain by either the Anunnaki archers or the worm we had encountered previously. Despite this, none of the survivors were disillusioned or ready to surrender. Indeed, they seemed instilled with a renewed resolve and strength, eager to continue the pursuit.

Most of the injuries suffered by our party were minor, except for one man named Oke, who had taken an arrow to the stomach. The shaft was embedded deep, and each time we tried to remove it, the barbed arrowhead did more internal damage. Sweating and pale, and squirming in agony, the anguished villager begged us to kill him so that he wouldn't further delay our rescue attempt. We conferred among ourselves, debating what to do. The wound was probably fatal, especially this far from the village, and Oke was obviously in a great deal of pain. While myself and several others debated a course of action, a villager named Tomkin, who I later learned had been the injured man's best friend since childhood, stabbed Oke in the heart with a dagger. It was quick and decisive, and Oke's final breath was spent thanking him. Tomkin wept when the deed was finished.

And then we were twelve. In addition to myself, Tolia, Karenk, Martek, and Tomkin, we had two other teens about Martek's age—Flik, a slender lad, and Sleeth, a girl who was as proficient with a sling as Tolia was with a bow. There were also three other men—a hunter named Kert, a farmer named Shlak, and a one-armed, one-eyed, grizzled old-timer named Trut, whose face was a mass of scar tissue. And there were two more women—another farmer named Marta and a young mother named Karune, whose child and sister were both among the captives.

We briefly mourned our dead and lamented that there was no time to bury them, or even cover their corpses to prevent animals from getting at them. Shlak and Marta seemed upset at the news of Apok's death, but they didn't question Tolia's account. The Anunnaki shaft jutting from his eye socket seemed to satisfy them. They didn't treat me with suspicion, and I saw no signs of dissent or argument from them.

One person who didn't lament Apok's passing was Trut. He stood over the corpse, scowling, while everyone else tended to their wounds and scavenged gear from our dead. When he was sure no one else was looking, the old man bent over and spat in Apok's face. Then he straightened up and noticed me watching him. He twitched with surprise.

"I take it you had no love for him?" I asked.

"Apok?" Trut glowered at me with his one eye. "No, I didn't. I see no point in lying about it. He was a snake—just like those we're tracking. Worse than them. I never liked him, even when he was a child. His mother should have strangled him with the birth cord and saved us all a lot of trouble."

"I didn't know him well, but that's the impression he left me with, too."

I walked over to him and stuck out my hand. Trut shook it. His palm was rough and hard, and he had the grip of a man thirty years his junior.

"You are not a snake, Aaron Pace. I like you."

"I'm sorry we've never had a chance to talk before now. I mean, I've seen you around the village, but ..."

"Oh, we've spoken on occasion. You just don't remember it. Kasheena's father introduced us when you joined the tribe. He was my best friend. I knew him since we were boys."

"Really?"

Trut nodded. "In fact, he's the reason I look the way I do."

"How's that?"

He pointed at Martek and Flik. "We were about their age. Out exploring, as young hunters do. We came upon a nest of fast lizards."

"Oh shit," I said. Fast lizards were what the people of the tribe called velociraptors.

"Aye. Indeed. There was a mother perched in the nest, guarding her young. The terrain was rocky and wet, and we were unfamiliar with the area. Kasheena's father had the misfortune to fall into the nest. I pulled him out just in time, and then the mother jumped me. The babies, perhaps following her lead, did the same."

He paused, cleared his throat, and spat again.

"What happened?" I asked.

"The mother took my arm off at the shoulder and her offspring chewed on my face before we managed to slay them all."

"I'm sorry."

"I'm not. I've earned many scars since then, in my travels, but these are my favorite, because I got them defending my friend."

"Your travels?"

He nodded again. "I've walked most of this land, exploring—searching for things that would help our tribe. Seeking knowledge."

"I've noticed you speak differently than the others. You almost sound like me."

He winked with his good eye. "I've picked up a thing or two. You're not the first outsider I've met, Aaron."

My astonishment must have been apparent, because Trut threw back his head and laughed. Until now, I'd had no idea anyone from the village had ever met someone from my world—or a parallel world like it. At that point during my time here, I'd only met one other castaway like me, and he was a cowboy from an alternate level where an apparent zombie outbreak had occurred in the Old West. I'd seen plenty of signs that others like myself had been here—abandoned airplanes, Nazi regalia, a wheelchair, articles of clothing, electronics, weaponry, and even a Jeep fused into the side of a cliff—but the cowboy had been the only living person, and he hadn't lived for long.

Of course, since then, I've met many like myself. One of them will figure into this story, and other stories to follow, provided I have the time and ability to write them all down for you.

Before Trut could elaborate more, the rest of our party gathered around us, looking expectant.

"We are ready, Aaron," Tolia said.

I nodded. "It's going to get harder to track them through this forest, and this delay has cost us more time. As long as we've got their trail, we're going to march hard. It might be a while before we break again. Carry only what you need, and keep up. If you fall behind, understand that we can't wait for you. Everybody clear?"

They nodded and murmured their consent. Martek stepped forward, holding the hilt of my sword out to me.

"You keep it," I said. "I'm sure you'll need it again before we're done."

"He wielded it well," Karenk boasted. "The boy cut those snake men down like they were weeds. I had thought to train him, but in truth, he is already skilled."

Martek smiled, but his expression was that of someone who might be feeling nauseous. He glanced at his feet and then back up at me. I held his gaze.

"Your first time killing?" I asked.

He shrugged. "I've killed for food but not ... not like today."

"Remember why we're doing this," I told him. "That makes it easier."

He nodded. "Thank you, Aaron."

I turned to Tolia. "Who's our best tracker?"

She pointed at Kert.

"I'm a hunter," he confirmed, "but Tolia is a better tracker than me."

"Let's use you both, then. You two take point. The rest of us will follow."

Tolia and Kert frowned.

"Point?" Tolia asked.

"He means you go first," Trut explained.

Tolia turned to me. "Then why did you not just say that?"

I grinned. "I thought I did. The two of you go ahead. We'll follow behind you at a safe distance, keeping you in sight. That way, you can track our enemies without us messing up the trail, and keep an eye out for any dangers."

Kert scratched his head. "Keep an eye ...?"

"Never mind," I said. "We've got a lot of lost time to make up for. Let's go."

We started our march through the forest, following about twenty yards behind Tolia and Kert. In the aftermath of the battle, the landscape was quiet, but as we continued onward, it began to come to life again. Birds chirped and sang above us, insects buzzed and flitted about, and small animals scurried unseen, hidden by the greenery. We had to narrow that distance some as the foliage grew denser around us. Even without Tolia and Kert's tracking abilities, I was able to follow the Anunnaki's passage. Broken twigs and flattened ferns and wildflowers were abundant, and the soil and leaves were disturbed by the tromping of many feet. But there were some areas—places where the ground became rockier and covered with stones—that the trail faded. At these times, our trackers would stop and confer, before unerringly leading us on in the right direction again.

We walked for what must have been several hours. It is always difficult to gauge the passage of time here, since the sun never sets, but I know that my feet began to hurt and my thirst grew. There were obvious signs that exhaustion was beginning to impact others among our group. They stumbled and slowed, sometimes straying from the path. Still, none of us dared call a halt. Eventually, I decided it was up to me. I was hesitant to do so, intent on making up for lost time and overtaking the kidnappers, but we wouldn't be much good if—once we encountered the Anunnaki—we were too tired to fight them.

I gave the order for a quick rest, and nobody argued. Indeed, many of them appeared quietly grateful for the brief respite. Some used the time to relieve themselves behind trees. Others ate and drank. The rest of us simply rested.

Martek and Flik sat with their backs against a tree trunk, legs splayed out in front of them. I stretched my aching joints and then plopped down beside them.

"Are you guys doing okay?" I asked.

They both nodded.

"All these trees ..." Martek gestured with a sweep of his arm. "I have never seen their like. I didn't notice them until after

Karenk and I had slain the snake men. Since then, I've been unable to notice anything else."

"Is this the furthest you've been from the village?"

"Yes," Flik answered. "We have hunted on the outskirts, of course. But beyond that ... we've just heard the stories."

"Trut told me he's done quite a bit of traveling."

"He is different," Flik confirmed. "More like you than the rest of us. Forgive me any offense, Aaron."

I smiled. "That's okay. I know what you mean."

Martek was still glancing around at all the foliage, his eyes wide with wonder. Then, he leaned forward and squinted off into the distance.

"What is that?"

Flik and I followed his gaze. I saw nothing out of the ordinary.

"What is what?" I asked, reaching for my weapon.

Instead of answering, Martek stood up and walked into the woods, his eyes focused intently. He stopped after about twelve feet and bent down. Then he began digging at the soil with the tip of his sword. Flik and I glanced at each other and then hurried to join him. Karenk and Trut, perhaps spotting the commotion, also wandered over.

"You're going to dull that blade," I warned, "and technically, it's still my sword."

"Yes, Aaron."

"Now, what are you—?"

I fell silent. Sticking out of the ground was a black tube made out of what looked like hard plastic. The end of it was tightly capped. Martek continued loosening the dirt around it. Then he grabbed it with one hand, tentatively at first, as if expecting an electrical shock or some other danger. When there was no reaction, he seized the tube with both hands and began to pull. When he had worked it free, he turned the cylinder over, studying it intently.

"What is it?" he asked.

"Let me see." I held out my hand.

Martek gave the tube to me, and I confirmed that it was indeed made out of durable plastic. I examined it closely, scrutinizing it for markings or a manufacturing stamp, but its black surface was smooth and featureless. It was undamaged, with no weathering, pocks, nicks, or scratches, despite the fact that it had been buried beneath the forest floor for who knew how long. After a moment, I tipped it over. Something rustled inside. I fiddled with the cap. The seal seamed tight and unbroken.

"Everybody move back a few steps," I cautioned.

Karenk frowned. "Why, Aaron? Is it dangerous?"

"I don't know. It could be. We don't know what's inside. If there is poison gas or some kind of toxin, I don't want to risk exposing the rest of you. So back away."

They immediately retreated to a safe distance, their expressions sober and apprehensive. I nodded at them, trying to project confidence, and then took a deep breath and held it. I slowly unscrewed the cap. When it was free and nothing had happened, I peered inside the tube. Then I tipped it over and the contents—a single sheet of rolled up paper—slid into my hand. The others hurried back over to my side, bristling with curiosity.

"What is it?" Flik asked.

I carefully unrolled the brittle, yellowed parchment, which was in much worse shape than its container. The group peered over my shoulder. The rest of our party began to wander over to us, as well.

I frowned. "I think it's a map, but I don't recognize any of this."

An artist of some talent had drawn different topography—trees and mountains and what I assumed must be lakes or some other type of bodies of water—but none of it seemed to match up with our current location. In the center of the map was something that looked like a giant cross, but its top and each of its arms had spheres attached to them. Judging by the scale, the object—whatever it was—must have loomed over the rest of the landscape. Tiny, squiggly lines radiated from it, as if to indicate the cross was glowing or shining or perhaps giving off heat. Written above the cross in faint, delicate penmanship were some Japanese letters that read:

出口

In the bottom right corner of the map, nearly concealed beneath my thumb and scrawled above a cluster of sketched trees, were more Japanese characters.

エントランス

"These markings are Japanese—a language from my world."

"What do they say?" Karenk asked.

"I don't know," I admitted. "It's a different language than the one I speak. Do any of you recognize any of these landmarks?"

They all shook their heads except for Trut, who pointed at the center of the map with one gnarled finger.

"I recognize the sword."

"Is that what that is? I thought it was a cross."

"Aye." He nodded. "It has been many years since I saw it with my own eye, but I'll never forget it. A giant sword, taller than any tree or mountain, standing in the middle of a great bowl-shaped valley, positioned almost directly beneath the sun. And when it flashes, the light is bright enough to blind you and incinerates anything in the valley. The ash and dust on the ground there are as deep as Karenk is tall."

"Do you mean when the sun flashes?" Martek asked. "I have never seen that."

"No, boy," Trut grumbled. "I mean when the sword flashes. Anything its light touches is instantly turned to dust."

I frowned. "And you're sure it's a sword?"

"I am. Though only a god or a giant could wield it. They say it guards a doorway—the passage from this world to all others. It strikes down any who try to use that door."

"But when I came here, I didn't see a giant sword. The doorway I used emerged into a jungle. That was where I met Kasheena and ... Bloop."

"That was an entrance, Aaron." Trut tapped the map again. "This is an exit. The Lost Level has many ways in, but only one way out—and that way is closed to all of us. The exit is not for us."

"Then who is it for?"

"I do not know."

I had no conscious desire to return to my Earth and my reality, yet I couldn't help but yearn to see it again, if only to glimpse something familiar. I guess it was nostalgia, but instead of thinking about a lover from the past or the halls of high school, I was remembering an entire planet and civilization. It also occurred to me that if Trut was incorrect—if we could, in fact, pass through this exit and travel back here again, I could better equip us against our enemy.

"How far away is it?" I asked. "This valley where you saw the sword."

Trut shook his head. "More steps than you can count. Your hair would be longer and your beard would be thicker and both would possibly show some gray by the time we reached it. As I said, I was there long ago. I'm not certain I could find it again so easily, even with the help of this map you've found."

Tolia stepped forward. "What are you thinking, Aaron? Your

brow is furrowed. What troubles you?"

"I was thinking that if this sword was close, and we could access that exit, I could travel back to my world and get us assistance—better weapons and things like that. But I guess it was a foolish idea."

"Aye," Tolia answered, lifting her bow. "It was. I have all the weapon I need here. Combined with the vengeance in my heart, it will do the job. We draw nearer to our loved ones, and I wish to slay more Anunnaki before this march has ended. Shall we continue?"

I nodded. "Yes. Same formation as before. You and Kert in the lead. The rest of us will follow. Everyone gather up your gear."

The group began to bustle about, doing as ordered. I tugged at Tolia's arm as she hurried past me. She arched one eyebrow, looking puzzled.

"Thank you," I whispered.

Her expression became even more confused. "For what, Aaron?"

"For being a leader ... and a friend. For not being afraid to disagree with me."

Slowly, she nodded. Then she smiled. "Somebody has to. I am happy to fulfill that role until Kasheena is safely with us again."

I chuckled as she walked away. Then I carefully rolled the parchment up and slid the map back into its protective case.

"Martek," I called, holding out the tube. "You found this. It's only right that you carry it."

"Are you sure, Aaron?"

I nodded. "Yes. But keep it safe. I'll wish to study it more when our rescue mission is completed. Okay?"

"You have my word. I shall guard it as I guard your sword."

We headed out again, back on the trail of our enemies. I

walked beside Trut. Our group maintained silence to better safeguard against the dangers of the forest and to conceal our pursuit, but I did pull Trut aside and whisper to him before focusing on our march.

"When this is over," I said, "I would like to hear more about your travels."

"It would be my pleasure. Although I should warn you, the tale is quite long."

I smiled. "I will make the time."

Lost in my own thoughts as we journeyed onward, I mulled over that statement—making time. What meaning did it have here, in a dimension where time itself was meaningless? Where living beings and artifacts from the past, present, and future existed simultaneously? Where terms like day and night had no meaning, other than in an abstract sense? I wished then that I could control the passage of time in the Lost Level, if only so we could catch up with Anunnaki, and I could be reunited with Kasheena again.

I hoped it wouldn't be much longer.

## [ 4 ]
## THE OLD MAN AND THE DINOSAUR

Tolia and Kert found the old man while the rest of us were trailing far behind. Deciding to sound the alert, Kert doubled back to our party. I stopped the procession when I saw him hurrying toward us. At first I thought they'd come upon the Anunnaki, or perhaps something big like a *Tyrannosaurus*, but then I noticed that his expression wasn't one of fear or alarm. It was more like bewilderment.

"What's wrong," I asked, "and where's Tolia?"

"She is up ahead," he said, "hidden in the undergrowth."

"Is everything okay?"

"There is a man ..."

"A man? Someone from our tribe?" The possibility occurred to me that perhaps one of the captives had escaped from the reptilians and was fleeing.

"No." Kert shook his head, and for a moment his expression turned sad. Then that confused look returned. "Someone else. He is ... like you, Aaron. But also not like you. And he is old, like Trut, but with more hair and both his eyes."

"Hair doesn't make the man," Trut grumbled, "and I can see better than two men with this one good eye."

Kert paused. "I meant no offense."

"Well, you damn sure caused it anyway."

"We don't have time for this," I scolded. "What is it about this old man that has you and Tolia so concerned, Kert? Is he armed?"

"No. But he is arguing with one of the horned beasts. Tolia believes he is a madman. She said to fetch you but leave the others behind, lest we capture his attention."

The horned beasts were what some among the tribe called triceratopses. If this old man was arguing with one, like Kert described, then Tolia was correct—he probably *was* insane.

"I agree," I said. "It's a good plan. Show me. The rest of you stay here."

"Are you sure?" Karenk asked.

"I am. If there's trouble, we'll shout for you."

"We will come running."

Kert crept forward, leading me through the forest. It occurred to me that we were now in a region I had never been to before. When Kasheena had first brought me to her village, it had been from a different direction. Since then, I'd been to the forest many times on hunting excursions and to get wood for fires and construction, but I'd never been this deep. I wasn't certain at this point that I would be able to find my way back to the village after we had rescued the captives. I could only hope the others had a better sense of direction. I found, for a long time during my stay here in the Lost Level, that my body and mind still relied on the directional concepts of north, south, east, and west. But those things don't exist here. Find a compass, or bring one in with you, and you'll discover that it is useless. The same goes for equipment and devices that rely on global positioning satellites or other directional services.

After a few minutes, Kert began to slow down. Soon enough,

I heard a voice—raspy and breathless, yet undeniably full of ferocity all the same.

"Away with you, now. I said scat, you fool thing!"

In response, something trilled and mewled. I recognized that sound. It was the same cry made by the baby triceratops's that Kasheena and I had encountered in this forest during our hunting trip. I wondered if this could be one of that same litter. It was a possibility, though, as I said before, we were much deeper into the woods than we had been during that ill-fated hunting trip.

Tolia was concealed so well that I didn't see her until we were right on top of her hiding place. She knelt in a cluster of tall ferns and was peering through them intently. Kert and I crouched down beside her, and I tapped her shoulder. Without speaking, she pointed through the fronds. I leaned forward, parted the ferns slightly, and looked where she had indicated.

Sure enough, there in a small clearing, stood a young triceratops—a little bigger than the babies Kasheena and I had discovered, but not by much. It was perhaps the size of a pony. Facing it stood an old man. I judged him to be in his early seventies. He had a thick, unruly crop of white hair, shot through with black, and was dressed in antiquated Civil War-era clothing—pants, white shirt, suspenders, and a black coat with tails. Dried mud clung to the pants' legs and the shirt was soiled with dirt and what appeared to be either blood or berry juice.

In the center of the clearing, a large gray boulder jutted at an angle from the ground. One side was sheer and flat and covered in primitive drawings. The old man had backed himself up against that flat side and was waving a tree branch at the triceratops, as if swiping at an insect with a flyswatter. But the branch sported green leaves, and the dinosaur clearly saw it as lunch, rather than a threat. The more the cantankerous senior swore at it, the more interested the toddler seemed to become. He swatted at it again, and the calf (because I suppose one could refer to a baby dinosaur as a calf) snatched the branch in its jaws and tugged playfully. The old man let go of his weapon, and the dinosaur munched happily.

"Go on now," the old man wheezed. "You've gotten what you wanted. Leave me be."

The triceratops stopped chewing and appeared to grow thoughtful. The calf tilted its head, gazing at him with big, black eyes. It started chewing again, slowly. Then, after swallowing the last of the leaves, the calf let out a series of 'meeps' and plodded forward.

Cornered, the geezer pressed himself against the etched rock. The dinosaur lowered its head and began to nuzzle the man's leg. Luckily, its horns were only tiny nubs. Trails of mucous glistened on the old man's pants as the creature rubbed its snout up and down, mewling with contentment. After a moment, the man reached down with one trembling hand and gave it a tentative pat on the head. When the dinosaur chirped in obvious delight, he scratched the bony plate between the creature's eyes.

"I used to believe that the most affectionate creature in the world was a wet dog," the old man murmured. The frustration in his voice was gone, replaced with a curious tenderness. "But you may be the second most affectionate. I shall have to reconsider everything I know about the universe and the place of man and dogs within it, and that is your fault."

I stood up slowly, holding out my empty hands to show that I meant no harm. Spotting me, the old man cried out in alarm. His friend snorted and turned, squealing at the intrusion.

"If I'm not mistaken," I said, "that little guy thinks you're his mother."

The old man straightened his posture and puffed out his chest. "Then you need a refresher in the aspects of biology, good sir, for I lack the genitalia necessary to be a mother, and this little guy, as you referred to her, is clearly a female."

I stifled a grin. "I stand corrected."

He eyed me warily. The triceratops stood at his side, head lowered.

"I warn you," the man said, "if you're a blackguard, then you are in for a fight."

"Are you going to feed me a tree branch, too?"

He balled his fists and raised them.

"Relax," I said, holding my hands high. "It was a joke. I mean you no harm."

He squinted his eyes and peered intently. "And what of your two companions, hidden there in the greenery like bandits?"

"They mean you no harm, either." I glanced down at them. "Tolia, Kert—put down your weapons. We're not out to hurt anybody."

"I am out to hurt the snake men," Tolia replied.

"Well, I think we can assume he's not one of them. Right?"

Both of them did as I'd commanded, and stood slowly, gaping at the old man and the dinosaur in wonder. He stared back, equally astonished.

"The three of you are dressed quite strangely," the man observed.

"I'm pretty sure my companions think the same of you."

"Perhaps. Still, I should seek a more suitable haberdashery, if I were you. Especially you, madam. I'm not certain I've ever seen animal fur like that."

"I'm not certain you've ever seen the animal the fur came from either," I said. "My name is Aaron Pace. This is Tolia and Kert."

"Why does he call me 'madam'?" Tolia whispered.

If the old man heard her, he gave no indication. Instead, he fished a white handkerchief from his pocket. The triceratops, mistaking it for some new, edible treat, darted for the cloth, but he waved it away.

"This is not for you," he scolded, and then turned his attention back to us. "Brevet Major Ambrose Gwinnet Bierce, at your service. Now that introductions have been made, and civility engaged, I wonder if you good people could tell me exactly where I am?"

"Ambrose Bierce?" I gasped. "The same Ambrose Bierce who wrote 'An Occurrence at Owl Creek Bridge'?"

Now it was the old man's turn to look puzzled. "I am indeed, sir. One and the same. Though, I must say, you have me at a disadvantage. It is somewhat of a rarity to meet an admirer of my fiction, rather than my journalism. I fear my attempts at stories are slated for permanent obscurity."

"Where I come from, your Civil War and horror stories are considered classics." I paused, and then added with some embarrassment, "I didn't even know you were a journalist."

"Really? You've not read *The Wasp*?"

I shook my head.

"*The San Francisco Examiner*? My series on the Railroad Refinancing Bill?"

"No, sorry."

"Surely, you are aware that a number of dunderheads in our country hold me responsible for inspiring the assassination of President McKinley with that absurd poem?"

Again, I shook my head. "No, sir. I don't know anything about that. I just know you for your fiction. Like I said, they're considered classics where I come from. We read them in school, and I liked them so much, I went out and found the rest."

Ambrose frowned. "To refer to something as a classic is to suggest that it stood the passage of time. Where do you come from, Mr. Pace, that they view my recent trifles of fiction as antiquity and teach it in school?"

"Minnesota."

"Indeed?" He glanced around at our surroundings. "This bears little resemblance to the Minnesota I remember."

"Oh, this isn't Minnesota."

"I should say not. I would be hard pressed to remember a rail journey from Mexico to Minnesota, especially given that until a few minutes ago, I was on the outskirts of Chihuahua. So, I ask you again—where am I?"

I sighed. "I'm afraid it's a long story. I'm happy to explain it to you, but we're in sort of a hurry. Some friends of ours were kidnapped, and we're tracking their captors. If you want to accompany us ...?"

"Young man, I barely know you."

"They have my child," Tolia said, her tone cold. "We do not have time for this, Aaron."

He waved the handkerchief dismissively. "Say no more. If these brigands are abducting children, then I will help you. If you'll have me, of course. I may be older, but I would dishonor my time with the Union Army's 9th Indiana Infantry Regiment if I did not accompany you."

I smiled. "We would be honored, sir. And I'll try to explain everything along the way. But I have to warn you, you might find the truth unbelievable at first."

"You aren't about to preach to me, are you? Tell me the good word about Jesus Christ and forgiveness and redemption? If so, I should warn you, I am an agnostic."

"No, Mr. Bierce, nothing like that. I'm not exactly a Christian, either."

"Good. Had you been a group of proselytizing Christians or Mormon missionaries, I would have had to seriously reconsider my offer of assistance. You don't have to be stupid to be a Christian, but it probably helps. Always going on about the Scriptures, and how they were divinely inspired. Holding that the sacred books of Christianity, which were cobbled together not long after we discovered the wheel, as supposedly distinguished from the false and profane writings on which all other faiths are based. As if believing in the blood of Jesus is any less ridiculous than believing in Bacchus, who our ancestors invented as a convenient excuse to get drunk. Proclaiming that any benighted creature who has the folly to worship something he can see and feel is a heathen. Preaching about the deliverance of sinners from the penalty of their sin through their murder of the deity against whom they sinned. The doctrine of redemption is the fundamental mystery of our holy religions, and whoso believeth in it shall not perish, but have everlasting life in which to try to understand it."

"Aaron," Tolia whispered. "The Anunnaki grow farther away, and so do Apotic and Kasheena and all the others."

Nodding, I lifted my finger to interrupt Ambrose, but he ignored me.

"No," he continued, "I have no use for any manmade religion. Religion is nothing but the bastard daughter of hope and fear—a way of explaining to the ignorant masses the nature of the unknowable, while controlling and robbing them."

I raised my hand, feeling like a student in a classroom. "Sir?"

"Cogito cogito ergo cogito sum. That's my motto. I think that I think, therefore I think that I am. That is as close to an approach to certainty as any priest or preacher or philosopher has yet made."

I raised my voice. "Mr. Bierce?"

He flinched, as if he had forgotten we were there. Beside him, the dinosaur mewled and rooted at the forest floor with her snout.

"I'm terribly sorry. Sometimes I do tend to pontificate."

"We have to go."

"Yes," he agreed, "let us be on our way."

I noticed that he was breathing heavily, and I could hear his lungs wheezing.

"Are you injured?" I asked.

Ambrose shook his head. "Just asthma. I'll be fine. I've suffered with it all my life."

"Is that blood on your shirt?"

"Hmmm?" He glanced down. "Oh, no. Not blood. When I woke up here, I was lying amidst some tiny berries. I'm afraid that in flailing around, I squashed them."

"Okay." I turned to Kert. "Go back and bring the others to us. Tolia and I will wait here with Mr. Bierce."

Nodding, he sprinted off into the greenery. Tolia and I waded out of the ferns and walked over to the center of the clearing. Tolia sighed, clearly unhappy with the delay. She eyed the baby dinosaur with suspicion and Ambrose with contempt. The triceratops cautiously trundled past us, giving Tolia and I both a wide berth, and then began eating our hiding place. She grunted happily, gorging herself on ferns.

"She seems to be very fond of those," Ambrose observed.

I noticed that his breathing had calmed somewhat, but he still seemed weak and somewhat bewildered.

"Are you sure you're okay, sir?"

He nodded. "I am. As I said, it is mostly my asthma. And my old war wounds ache. But if you get to be my age, everything aches, really. I'll be fine."

I knew that in my world, a seventy-one-year-old Ambrose Bierce had left Washington D.C. in October 1913 for a tour of the battlefields he'd fought on during the Civil War. After visiting Louisiana, he'd reached El Paso, Texas by that December, and traveled into Mexico, which was then experiencing a violent revolution. He had joined up with Pancho Villa's army, serving as an observer, and was there for the battle of Tierra Blanca. He'd ridden with Villa's forces as far as Chihuahua and disappeared soon after, vanishing without a trace. Researchers and historians had proffered a number of theories as to what had happened to him, including execution by firing squad there in Chihuahua as punishment for Bierce's criticisms of Villa himself. I wondered if his disappearance had been the work of the Lost Level and the mysterious forces and energies that reside in this place.

"How long have you been here?" I asked. "And how did you get here?"

"Well, you still haven't explained to me where here is, but to answer your question, I was in my room in the city of Chihuahua. My asthma was being quite a bother, and I was exhausted. I wrote a letter to my dear friend, Blanche Partington, and afterward, I decided to get some sleep. I was so tired that I decided not to bother with changing into my nightclothes. When you get to be my age, such social concerns don't really matter. I left instructions with my secretary and traveling companion, Carrie, to wake me at sunrise. Instead, I woke here. I don't know how long I slept. Indeed, I am not yet convinced that I am awake, given the nature of this place, and of that fern-gobbling thing over yonder, and your appearance here. But, dream or reality, I would guess I have been here but a short time. Perhaps ten minutes passed before your rather fortuitous arrival."

"And you woke up here, in this clearing?"

"Indeed. Lying prone on the ground over there, as I said." He pointed to the edge of the clearing, covered with short, stunted greenery and a patch of tiny strawberries. At least, they looked like strawberries. But given the fact that the baby triceratops was ignoring them in favor of the ferns, I suspected they weren't edible.

I walked over to the boulder he'd been standing against and inspected the crude pictographs. Someone had etched them into the surface and then painted the lines with red and orange hues to make them stand out more. Although I was certainly no expert, the carvings didn't seem that old to me. There was no sign of fading or wear, and nothing to indicate long-term exposure to the elements. They depicted a group of humanoids hunting what appeared to be a unicorn. Another set showed those same humanoid figures dancing around a fire. There were other representations, as well. These were mostly random animals, including an octophant. I wondered who had etched these into the stone. If this particular forest had a tribe living beneath its trees, we had never encountered them or seen signs of their existence. And the designs were too crude to have been fashioned by Kasheena's people. I wondered if the pictographs had been carved somewhere else—another dimension—and had then been transported here. Not for the first time, I found myself wondering about the rocks and soil and minerals that made up the Lost Level. While most of the flora and fauna that inhabited this place had originally come from elsewhere, could the same be said of the dirt beneath our feet? I had seen oddly colored rocks and stones before that I'd been unable to identify. Did everything in this place—with the exception of those generations who were born here—come from somewhere else? And if so, then what was the Lost Level's primal form?

Now, of course, I am an old man, and know the answer to many of those mysteries, but were I to recount them all for you here and now, I would fill these accounting ledgers and have no space to finish this particular tale.

The baby triceratops had nearly finished eating all of the ferns. Tolia shifted uneasily from foot to foot, clearly anxious and annoyed. Ambrose rested, patiently waiting and watching as I examined the pictographs. Before I had a chance to study them further, Kert returned with the rest of our tribe. Tolia let out an exaggerated sigh.

"Finally," she exclaimed, "we can be off."

"We can," I agreed. "Mr. Bierce, if you'll walk with me, I'll try to fill you in on everything. I'll warn you, though, we may have a long march ahead of us before we rest again."

"Camels and Christians accept their burdens kneeling. I shall accept mine on my feet. Lead on, Mr. Pace."

"You'll need some weapons."

I handed him my dagger and its sheath, as well as the rusty box cutter I'd stored in my gear. He accepted both of them gratefully, and examined the latter with some curiosity. After a moment, he figured out how to operate it, extending the razor blade and then retracting it. He did this several times, obviously delighted.

I suggested to Kert and Tolia that they take a break and let some of our other trackers take over as point in the procession. Kert agreed, unable to hide the gratitude on his face. The young man was obviously tired. Tolia, however, refused, insisting that she was fine for the job. Rather than arguing with her, I agreed. But I did pull her aside before we departed.

"Don't overdo it," I cautioned. "Think of Apotic. He's going to want his mother after we've rescued him."

"I shall not fail my own son."

"All the more reason not to overexert yourself. We'll need you in fighting shape when we catch up with the Anunnaki."

"I could fight them in my sleep."

"I'd much rather you fight them on your feet, Tolia. Remember, some of our friends here are just farmers and seamstresses. Not all of them are warriors like you. We're going to need you if we are to succeed in rescuing our loved ones."

Nodding, Tolia touched my shoulder and squeezed. "I understand, Aaron. I promise to save most of my fight for the battle to come."

"Fair enough."

Tolia and Kert's replacement—who turned out to be Shlak—headed out, back on the trail of the snake men. The rest of us followed along behind them. I asked Karenk to bring up the rear of the procession, hoping his considerable size and saber-tooth tiger-skull helmet would act as a deterrent to anything creeping up behind us. Well, perhaps not a full-grown Tyrannosaurus rex or a twenty-foot tall, laser-equipped death robot, but you get the idea.

But as it turned out, Karenk wasn't the deterrent I'd hoped for, because as we made our way through the forest, something cried out behind us. The group turned, weapons drawn, as Ambrose's baby triceratops burst from the foliage, half-chewed fern leaves still jutting from the corners of her mouth. Her little legs pumped as she hurried to catch up with us, mewling loudly. The tribe parted, clearing a path. Ignoring them, the dinosaur wobbled up to Ambrose and snorted, giving him kisses with her snout. Glistening trails of mucous covered his pants and shirt as she trilled happily. Sighing, Ambrose reached down and patted her head.

"I think you've made a friend," I said, grinning.

"Indeed," he replied.

"We're not going to be able to sneak up on the Anunnaki with her squealing," Trut warned.

"She only squeals when Ambrose gets too far away," I pointed out, crouching down on my haunches to scratch the bony plate atop her head. Cooing, the dinosaur turned her attention away from Ambrose and tried to lick me instead. Her tongue was slimy and yet rough like sandpaper. Flies buzzed around her hindquarters, and black gook crusted the corners of her eyes. I reached out slowly with one hand, speaking soothingly, and cleaned some of it away. Then I stood up again.

"She's going to need a name."

Ambrose nodded. "Agreed, although I am hard pressed to come up with something suitable."

"How about Squeaker?" Trut suggested.

I smiled. "How about Fern? You know, like from *Charlotte's Web*? They seem to be her favorite food, after all."

"Fern is an excellent choice," Ambrose agreed. "Although I am not familiar with this Charlotte you mention."

"I guess you wouldn't be," I admitted. "That came after your time. It was a book."

"You can tell me all about it," Ambrose suggested, "after you've explained to me where I am and what is happening."

We began hiking again. Ambrose and I fell back to the rear, alongside Karenk, so that Fern could keep up. She trundled along at his side, grunting and cooing, apparently happy to be a part of the procession. And that was how our determined dozen became fourteen again.

Unfortunately, those numbers didn't last long.

# [ 5 ]
# THAT'S SOME PIG

In school, I had learned that Ambrose Bierce had a sardonic, sarcastic view of human nature and that his motto had been "Nothing Matters." I found the real-life incarnation of him to be very similar to what I had been taught. While perhaps not a complete nihilist, he certainly had no use for religion, occultism, or mysticism. And yet, despite that, he listened with interest and respect as I explained everything to him—the Labyrinth, the Lost Level, the details of my arrival here and what I had learned and experienced since. He didn't interrupt me or ridicule my account. Instead, he listened with rapt, professional attention. I could tell by his facial expressions that his keen mind was analyzing everything I said, weighing it against his own experiences thus far and on the evidence around him. The telling took a long while, and I was exhausted by the time I finished.

"So," I asked, "what do you think?"

He was silent for a long moment, and I began to wonder if he was going to answer me at all. Then Ambrose cleared his throat and swept his hand from side to side, indicating the forest surrounding us.

"The last thing I remember before waking here was falling asleep. Thus, it would be easy for me to believe that this is all a dream, but I've never known dreams—even the most vivid ones—to be this detailed. I can smell the shit on Fern's flanks, feel the breeze on my skin, and hear my chest rumble with this damned asthma. Every injury I've ever received pains me right now. Mind you, I'm not referring to phantom pains or twinges. I can feel the ache deep in my bones. That doesn't happen in dreams. One doesn't feel pain in dreams, nor does one smell shit. So, I do not believe I am dreaming."

"Then, what do you believe?"

"I believe in myself. I believe that I am an intelligent man. In our civilization, and under our republican form of government—or at least the civilization and government that existed in my time—intelligence is so highly honored that it is rewarded by exemption from the cares of office. That is why I have never held office and never will. History is an account, mostly false, of events, mostly unimportant, which are brought about by rulers, mostly knaves, and soldiers, mostly fools. So, when you tell me that this strange land I've found myself in is full of artifacts from history—both the past and the future, and not just from our world—I trust my intelligence. It is in my nature to treat all things divine or supernatural with marked respect, in that I prefer to not have anything to do with them. And yet, nothing else seems to account for my being here. I never believe anything without evidence, but the evidence is all around me. Some of the trees are familiar. Others are unlike anything I have ever seen before. Indeed, I am hard pressed to imagine that some of them could have ever flourished on Earth. I've noted the sun's position in the time we've walked, and it hasn't moved. And then there's this."

He reached down and patted the baby triceratops. She cooed, almost lovingly.

"Fern certainly didn't exist in my time," he continued.

"Therefore, I am inclined to believe you, Aaron. Understand, that is a difficult thing for me to do, and perhaps even more difficult to admit out loud. Trust in my fellow man is not something that comes easily to me. As a rule, I do not trust humanity without collateral security. I've found that it hurts no one to be treated as an enemy entitled to respect until he shall prove himself a friend worthy of affection. And yet, I sense no animosity or trickery in your words, nor in the actions of your fellow men and women. Indeed, judging by the demeanor of ... what was her name?"

"Tolia?"

He nodded. "Yes, Tolia. I dare say she has the look and tone not just of a woman anxious for revenge, but of a mother desperate to save her child. And that desperation extends to the rest of your party, as well. They all have that same haunted demeanor. I have seen it many times before, on many different battlefields. As loathe as I am to admit it, and as fantastical as some of your story sounds, I choose to believe it. All of it. Though I still do not understand how I came to be here."

"I don't either," I admitted.

"Perhaps when I next sleep, I'll wake up back in Mexico."

"Maybe ... but I don't think it works like that. At least, it hasn't for me."

We talked more as we walked. One thing I was curious about was whether or not this Ambrose Bierce was from my level—my Earth—or some alternate reality version. I asked him questions about his life to help me determine that. He'd been born into poverty in 1842 (he joked that his parents were poor because they were honest) in a log cabin in the backwoods of Ohio. He had thirteen brothers and sisters, all of whom had names beginning with the letter A—Abigail, Amelia, Ann, Addison, Aurelius, Augustus, Almeda, Andrew, Albert, and so on. He'd left home at the age of fifteen and found work at a small Ohio newspaper. As a member of the Union Army's 9th Indiana Regiment during the Civil War, he'd fought in the battles of Western Virginia, Philippi, Rich Mountain, and Shiloh. It was the latter that had inspired several of his short stories. He'd also suffered a serious head wound during the Battle of Kennesaw Mountain, which he illustrated to me by pulling his hair back and showing me a horrific scar. After the war, he had worked primarily as a journalist and writer, but had also briefly tried his hand at mining in the Dakota Territory.

He mentioned having been married, and that he'd had three children, but Ambrose refused to say more about them—instead falling into a rant about the insects in the forest—and I decided not to press him about them. Clearly, he didn't wish to discuss his family, and I suspected why. On my world, Ambrose Bierce and his wife, Mollie, got divorced after he found evidence of adultery in the form of compromising letters to her from an admirer. She'd died not long after. Both of his sons had died, as well. The youngest, Leigh, had died from complications of pneumonia related to alcoholism. The oldest son, Day, had committed suicide after being spurned by a lover.

I gently turned the conversation to his written works. The bibliography he recited seemed to match up with what I remembered from school—*The Devil's Dictionary*, weird fiction stories like "An Occurrence at Owl Creek Bridge," "The Death of Halpin Frayser," and "The Damned Thing," and of course his war stories like "The Boarded Window," "Chickamauga," and "Killed at Resaca."

Eventually, I was fairly certain that he had indeed come from my Earth, and yet, having originated in a time nearly a hundred years before my birth, he had arrived here after me. This was similar to a previous encounter I'd had in the Lost Level when Bloop and I had come across an Old West cowboy from an alternate reality. In his case, I'd known for sure it was an alternate reality, rather than my world, because he'd spoken of a zombie pandemic that had infected the country. In Ambrose's case, everything seemed to match up to what I knew of him from a historical perspective. The only thing I was uncertain about was that he mentioned a friendship with the poet and writer Stephen Crane. I was aware of Crane, certainly. We'd read the obligatory *The Red Badge of Courage* in school, but more than that, his poem "In the Desert" was a personal favorite of mine. Still, I couldn't remember ever having heard of a friendship between the two men in my reality.

Our conversation returned to me again, or more specifically, my time with the tribe and my relationship with Kasheena. I told him about how we'd met and of all the times she had saved my life. Oblivious to the other tribe members within earshot, I found myself confiding in him about my hopes with her for the future—and my fear that the Anunnaki had taken that future away from us. My voice choked with emotion, and before I could stop myself, I began to weep. Warm tears, born out of anger and hatred and fear coursed down my face. I wiped my eyes and nose with the back of my hand, took a deep breath, and muttered an apology.

"I cried for my parents." Karenk clapped his big hand on my shoulder and squeezed. "You have nothing to be sorry for."

"He is correct," Ambrose agreed. "I've always felt that, for myself at least, love is nothing more than a temporary insanity that is curable by marriage. But it is clearly evident you love this woman. Don't be ashamed. You have nothing to apologize for. And besides, it's a known fact that women in love are less ashamed than men. They have less to be ashamed of."

Nodding, I thanked them both. We walked on in silence for a while. Ambrose wheezed frequently, but other than that, he seemed capable of continuing the hike. Fern grunted at the old man's side, occasionally pausing to root at the ground with her snout, and then galloping along to catch back up with him again. Karenk remained quiet, keeping his attention focused on the terrain, alert for any possible threats.

Further ahead, the rest of the party remained quiet, as well. Only the younger rescuers—Martek, Flik, and Sleeth—showed any sign of frivolity. While everyone else was serious and dour, those three remained relatively upbeat and energetic, if somewhat tired. I also noticed that both Flik and Sleeth seemed to be attracted to Martek. The hapless youth was apparently oblivious to the attentions of both, treating them as friends.

Of us all, it was Karune who seemed the most desperate. She plodded along at the head of the procession, following the trail blazed by Tolia and Shlak. It was clear to me that the young mother was exhausted, but—anxious to save her child and sister—she asked for no rest, and maintained a steady, almost punishing pace.

Eventually, the forest began to thin. The trees grew farther apart, allowing more sunlight to filter down through their boughs. In turn, the undergrowth began to thicken, slowing our progress as we picked our way around thorn bushes and vines. We saw a patch of razor grass—a deadly plant that grew plentifully in most of the Lost Level's climes—but Tolia and Shlak had marked it and our group easily avoided it, skirting the edges. In the center of the patch lay the partial skeleton of some hapless animal, the mottled bones gray and white against the deep green.

Ambrose's asthma grew worse. Tomkin stumbled, caught himself, and brushed off Kert when the younger man reached out to help him. A few minutes later, it was Kert's turn to lose his footing. Soon after, I heard Karenk stifling a yawn behind me. As for myself, my feet ached and my eyes were beginning to burn. Realizing that we needed rest, no matter what, I began looking for a suitable place to make camp. When we came to another clearing, I decided it was as good a spot as any.

"Okay," I said, raising my voice so they'd all hear me. "Let's stop here. Karune, can you run ahead and let Tolia and Shlak know?"

Nodding, she darted down the trail, disappearing into the trees. When she returned with them a few minutes later, it was clear from Shlak's expression that he was grateful for the break. Tolia and Karune, on the other hand, seemed pensive and impatient, despite their obvious fatigue. I motioned at everyone to join me in the center of the clearing. One by one, they gathered around, huddling in the grass, except Fern, who found something interesting to eat.

"I know what some of you are thinking," I said. "That we shouldn't stop. That we should press on and catch up to our loved ones. Believe me, there's a big part of me that would like to do the same. But the fact of the matter is we're all tired. We've been on the move since the village was attacked—hiking and running and fighting without many breaks. If we don't get some rest, we won't be any good to our loved ones when we do eventually catch up with them."

Tolia shook her head. "With respect, Aaron, we may not catch up with them at all if we don't quicken our pace."

"Have you seen signs that we're getting closer?"

She hesitated, her eyes darting to Kert and Shlak. "Yes."

"Okay, then. The snake men have to sleep sometime, too. And even if they don't, their captives will need to. They didn't go through all this trouble of attacking our village and kidnapping our loved ones just to let them die during a forced march. And remember, they probably think we all got killed in that ambush back at the start of the forest. I'm betting they'll rest soon, too. We'll each get a short amount of sleep—just enough that we're not falling over on our faces— and then we'll continue on. Any objections?"

There were none, so I gave orders for some of them to gather dead wood and build a campfire, and others to prepare some food. I posted four guards, one on each side of the clearing. Those who didn't have a task were given the job of caring for our gear and weapons—sharpening blades, making sure arrows were still threaded, and the like. They bustled about, content to have a task to focus on. I was impressed to see Ambrose pitching in to help, carrying armfuls of kindling back to the center of the clearing. His wrinkled old brow glistened with sweat, but he didn't complain. Indeed, he seemed happy to help.

We kept the fire small—enough to cook our meal and ward off potential predators, but not enough to signal the Anunnaki that we were nearby. The tribe members had been clever enough to gather wood that gave off relatively little smoke when burned. We sat around it, eating together, and I had portions taken to the guards. The kindling popped and crackled, and the heat seeped into my feet, and then my legs, and then throughout my body. Yawning, I blinked my eyes.

"It's strange," Ambrose mused, peering up at the sun and shading his eyes with one gnarled hand. "My body tells me it's after midnight, yet the sun is still at high noon. I fear I'll never sleep again under these conditions."

I shrugged. "You'll get used to it"

"I hope you are right."

At the insistence of the others, I stayed awake long enough to tell them an abbreviated version of the story of *Charlotte's Web*. It was easy enough to edit the story for the tribe. I just changed the details to things they'd understand—the county fair became a harvest festival, and instead of a rat, Templeton became a Slukick. By the time I was finished, half the party had fallen asleep. I had four of them replace the guards, and told them to wake another shift of replacements when they got tired.

Ambrose recited some poetry and quotations from *The Devil's Dictionary* for those who were still awake. I imagine that most of the meaning must have gone over my friends' heads, but they still listened with interest, their unabashed curiosity with the old man not yet slaked. He stood near the fire, one hand behind his back, the other resting lightly on Fern's head, and spoke in a quiet but clear voice.

The last thing I heard him say before I drifted off was, "Immortality is a toy which people cry for, and on their knees apply for, dispute, contend, and lie for, and if allowed would be right proud to eternally die for ..."

Kasheena was there with me, in my dreams. I promised that I'd find her soon, and that I would die for her, die for her eternally, but she just laughed at me and danced away.

# [ 6 ]
# THE VENUS FLY TREE

I woke to Kasheena nuzzling my ear. Her breath was warm but made me shiver with delight. It felt wonderful—that simple touch, that human contact. I stirred, and as she continued, another part of me stirred, as well. Eyes still closed, I chuckled and sighed. My skin prickled with goosebumps.

"Mmmm," I murmured. "I missed you."

She responded by licking me. As I began to awaken more, I realized that her tongue felt ... sticky. I caught a whiff of something then—something that smelled like a cross between a dog's breath and rotting vegetation. A second later, I remembered that Kasheena was among the captives—and even if she hadn't been, she'd always smelled much nicer than this. Her breath had never been this warm. And her saliva had never been sticky.

I opened my eyes and groaned, recoiling in disgust as Fern licked my forehead with her long, gray tongue. Glistening with ropy white strands of foamy saliva, it looked like a piece of raw liver and had the sandpaper consistency of a cat's tongue. Cringing, I waved the baby dinosaur away and sat up. When I wiped my face, my hands came away slimy. Fern snorted, pawing at the ground.

I glanced around the camp, expecting to hear laughter or taunts from my companions, but everyone else was still asleep, with the exception of Karenk, Tolia, Flik, and Marta, who were on guard duty and staring out into the forest. The fire had died down to nothing more than embers and ash. A thin wisp of smoke curled from it, dissipating before it got even a few feet off the ground.

Fern tried to nuzzle me again. I pushed her away, gently but firmly. She grunted in protest.

"Get," I whispered. "Scat!"

She tilted her head, staring at me with those huge, soft black eyes, and then farted. Her nub of a tail wiggled like a pig's. Chuckling, I reached out and patted her head.

"You're a cute little thing, but you stink. Now go wake up Ambrose, okay?"

Fern waddled off, almost as if she'd understood me, and turned her affections to the old man, who was sleeping on the ground nearby, his legs curled up to the point that his knees almost touched his chest. At some point, he'd taken off his coat and wadded it up to use as a pillow. I felt sorry for him. Yesterday, he'd been asleep in a hotel bed. Now, he was sleeping in the rough and the nearest hotel was a dimension away. At his age, the ground had to be painful. I was sore and aching. I could only imagine how he would feel when he awoke.

I stretched, working out the kinks in my back and neck, and then whistled to catch the attention of the four guards. They wandered over to me, while a few of our other tribe members began to slowly stir.

"Did you get any sleep at all?" I asked Tolia.

She shrugged. "Some. You were right with what you said. I'll be of no use to anyone if I am tired and weak. But my anger ... my anger does not make for a good pillow, Aaron. When I close my eyes, I see Heresh, legless and bleeding, crawling after our son. When my eyes are open, I hear Apotic calling me, like a phantom. But I am rested and ready to march."

"I understand that this is hard," I said. "The waiting, I mean. If you're up to it, why don't you and Kert get a head start on us. Get back on the trail. Mark it for us like you did yesterday. We'll catch up as soon as everybody is awake."

Tolia nodded. "Thank you, Aaron."

"Kert, is that okay with you?"

"Yes, Aaron. I am anxious to start again, as well." He turned to Tolia. "I will fetch our gear."

The two of them hurried off while the rest of the encampment woke. Some wandered off to relieve themselves while others stoked the fire and prepared a quick breakfast. Ambrose rose slowly, grunting and huffing. He supported himself by leaning against Fern and wobbling to his feet. It was obvious that he was in pain, but it was also obvious he was trying not to let on about it.

"I'm sorry about the accommodations," I apologized. "The ground doesn't make for a good bed. When we get back to the village, we'll fix you up with some much better sleeping arrangements."

He nodded. "I'm surprised I slept at all, what with that damnable sun shining the entire time. How anyone here can make it through the night is beyond me."

"They—the ones who were born here—have no concept of night, really."

"And what of government or religion? Do they have concepts of those?"

"Not like you and I know them."

Ambrose grinned. "Well, then. Perhaps I will like it here after all."

I was distracted for a moment by laughter. I glanced toward the campfire and saw Martek, Flik, and Sleeth giggling together over some shared joke. When I turned back to Ambrose, he was flexing his fingers and wincing.

"Is the pain bad?" I asked.

He waved his hand dismissively. "The pain is what it is. When you get to be my age, there is always some level of pain, even while you are sleeping. You learn to live with it. Indeed, quite often I forget about it entirely. It is far easier to ignore pain than it is an empty stomach. What I could do with is some breakfast."

I nodded toward the campfire. "They'll take care of you. I've got to see to preparations."

"You are anxious to depart."

"I am. We're going to have to speed up our pace today."

"Then I had best get ready."

He began stretching and turning, easing out his aches. Fern stood by his side, watching. Then, growing bored with his calisthenics, she wandered across the clearing and began to eat. After a few moments, Ambrose joined the others around the fire and did the same. Our meal consisted of Slukick and some edible leaves—two things the old man was unaccustomed to. He eyed both suspiciously at first, but then devoured them with gusto.

When everyone was finished, we started off again, following the trail. Once more, Tolia and Kert had left marks on the trees, so it was easy enough to track them. We kept a steady pace, and I was worried for a bit that it might be too punishing for Ambrose, but he kept up with the rest of us and didn't complain. Indeed, he didn't seem to notice it at all. His attention was focused instead on our surroundings. He studied everything—the flora and fauna, the rocks and minerals and soil, the sky and the sun, cloud movements, and even my fellow tribe members. He didn't ask any questions because he'd said that talking for an extended period of time while simultaneously exerting himself made his asthma worse, but I suspected he was noting everything he observed for later analytical study.

"You say the sun never moves?" he asked at one point.

I confirmed that it didn't.

"So that would indicate this planet doesn't rotate. There are weather patterns—wind and cloud movement—and gravity, and yet the planet does not rotate. What if it is not a planet at all?"

"I don't believe it is," I replied. "The Lost Level occupies a dimensional space, but there's no reason that the particular space it occupies needs to be a planet."

"And yet, it has its own solar body and its own atmosphere."

"Correct."

"Have you ever wondered what is up there, beyond the sun? If space, as we know it, exists beyond a planet's boundaries, then what exists beyond the edges of a dimension such as this?"

I opened my mouth to respond, but no answer was forthcoming. Ambrose laughed.

"It's a rhetorical question, Aaron. No need to bother yourself. But I should imagine it is but the first of many questions that I will ponder on however many sunlit nights I remain in this place."

The forest thinned more, and the ground began to slope downward. We soon caught up with Tolia and Kert at the edge of a dry creek bed. They stood on its bank, hovering over a ten-foot drop. Kert had one hand wrapped around a low-hanging tree branch about the thickness of his arm. Oddly, Tolia's dagger seemed to be embedded in the same limb. As we approached, he and Tolia turned in our direction. I could see from their expressions that something was wrong.

"What is it?" I asked. "What's the matter?"

Tolia's tone was alarmed. "We were about to cross this ravine.

Kert grabbed onto that branch to steady himself, and now he cannot let go."

"Why not?"

"The tree will not allow him to."

I glanced at Kert. His expression was calm—the serenity a stark contrast to Tolia's demeanor. When I reached for the tree branch, Tolia stopped me.

"No, Aaron. Don't touch it. The tree is sticky, like a spider's web. You can see what happened to my dagger when I tried to cut through it."

I looked again at her weapon, and realized then that the blade wasn't embedded in the wood—it was stuck fast, as if it had been glued to the tree.

"What the hell?" I muttered.

"All of the tree's bark is like that," Tolia said. "I have never encountered anything like this."

The rest of the group had clustered around us, keeping their distance from both the tree and the edge of the gulley. I glanced back at them.

"How about the rest of you? Ever seen anything like this? Trut, how about in your travels?"

The others shook their heads, but Trut lowered his.

"I have," he said, his voice grave. "And it has never ended well."

"What is it?" I asked.

Trut shrugged. "I don't know the name for it, but I have seen this type of tree before. Their sap is like glue—unbreakable. Were Kert able to tear himself free, the damage he'd suffer in the process would be severe. His skin would rip and tear. Possibly the muscles beneath his skin, as well. The process could kill him. But he won't free himself."

"Why not?"

He nodded at Kert. "See how content he is? I've heard these

trees have that effect on their victims. It keeps them calm and happy."

"Some type of hallucinogen?" I asked.

"Delivered chemically through the sap," Ambrose said.

Trut nodded. "Perhaps, Mr. Bierce. While I have knowledge of your world, and other worlds, I can't be sure. But I suspect you are guessing, the same as me."

"I am," Ambrose admitted.

"We definitely don't have anything like this on Earth," I agreed. "Kert, are you okay? How do you feel?"

He glanced over his shoulder at me, smiling widely. Drool dribbled down his chin. His eyes had a glazed, glassy look. Despite the heat, he was shivering. When he spoke, his voice was slurred.

"I am fine, Aaron. It tingled at first, but now it is nice. I wish to stay right here."

"No can do, buddy. Just stick tight. We'll figure something out."

"A rather poor choice of words," Ambrose muttered.

"You're the writer," I responded. "Just make sure you keep Fern away from it. The last thing we need is her trying to eat that thing."

"It will be the other way around," Trut muttered. "The sap holds the tree's victims in place while it slowly digests them."

The group expressed horror at this prospect, but Kert seemed oblivious to the danger he was in.

I walked around and studied the tree. It had a thick, solid trunk and an abundance of low-hanging limbs. If the branches were coated with sap, it was undetectable to my eye. Further up, there was a canopy of waxen-hued leaves. I noticed a bird skeleton dangling from one branch up high. I stared at it, bobbing in the breeze, and shuddered.

"Shlak," I called, "we need your axe."

He stepped forward and nodded. "I do not fear it, Aaron."

"It won't do any good," Trut said.

"We have to try," I answered.

Without a word, Shlak adopted a stance next to the tree. Then, with both hands, he raised the weapon over his head and swung. The axe arced downward and struck the limb just a few inches from Kert's fingers. Instead of chopping into the wood, there was a dull *thunk,* and the axe didn't move. Cursing, Shlak locked his knees and pulled. The axe remained stuck fast. He pulled harder, grunting, but still the weapon didn't budge. The tendons strained in his neck and he leaned to one side, perhaps to get a better grip. We all gasped as Shlak's arm brushed against the tree trunk. He immediately stopped, eyes wide with fear.

"I cannot move my arm," he whispered, letting go of the axe handle. "Help me! My arm is stuck."

Everyone began to surge forward, jostling Tolia and me. I fought to retain my balance, nearly bumping into Shlak. He whimpered in fear.

"Stay back," I ordered. "Everybody stay back!"

"Get that shirt off of him," Trut urged, "before the sap seeps through to his skin."

Shlak wore pants and a long-sleeved shirt fashioned from animal skins. As soon as Trut spoke, he began twisting around, trying to loosen himself.

"Hold on," I told him. "Let me untie you. Slowly ... don't rush."

"We have to be quick," he panted. "I am starting to feel it. It ... tingles."

I hurried to undo the leather straps that tied his shirt together. Groaning, Shlak slipped free of the garment and lunged forward into my arms, trembling against me. We both stumbled backward. He caught himself and stood upright, examining his arm and gasping from fear. Shlak was covered in thick, black body hair, but there was now a bald spot on his forearm where the hair had ripped free. Little drops of blood welled up from his pores.

Kert laughed. His face had a dreamy, careless expression. He reached for the tree limb with his free hand, but Tolia grabbed his arm and wrestled it away.

Karenk clasped Shlak's shoulder and asked, "Are you okay?"

"Yes." Shlak nodded. "I am now. It felt ... good. Natural. For just a second, when the sap seeped through my shirt and onto my arm, it tingled and I wanted to feel more."

"That explains Kert's behavior," I said. "The chemical effect must be consistent."

Kert giggled again, nodding vigorously. "Let me be a part of the tree, Aaron."

"We are wasting time again," Tolia said, gazing off into the distance.

"We can't just leave him here," I argued.

Tolia didn't reply. I glanced around at the others. They all stared at me, waiting for a decision.

"Some of you grab his legs," I said. "Tolia, keep hold of his arm. Karenk, you're the strongest. I want you to grab his wrist, just below where he's stuck. Be careful you don't get stuck, too."

I encircled Kert's waist with my arms while the others took their positions. When they were ready, I nodded.

"On the count of three. One ... two ... THREE!"

We tugged and Kert screamed. I stared in horror as the skin on his palm and fingers stretched like taffy and then began to split and tear. Blood gushed out from the wounds and dripped down onto Karenk, but still Kert remained stuck fast.

"More," I urged, raising my voice to be heard over Kert's anguished shrieks.

We pulled harder, straining with the effort. Kert's complexion went white and he bit through his bottom lip. The cords in his neck strained and bulged. His screams grew even more frantic as the skin on his wrist, just above Karenk's grip, began to stretch and tear.

"Enough," I shouted. "Stop! We keep this up, we're going to skin him alive."

We relaxed our grip and Kert sagged in our arms, breathing heavily. His eyes were closed. His blood coated the tree limb and spattered onto the forest floor. He moaned, chest heaving. Then, he opened his eyes again and his expression changed from anguish to delight.

"There," he panted. "The tree is making it better again ..."

"Hold him," I said to Tolia. "Don't let him get his other arm stuck."

I led the others away, out of Kert's earshot.

"I warned you," Trut said.

Ignoring him, I looked at the others. "Do any of you have an idea?"

They murmured among themselves, but it was clear that no solutions were forthcoming. None of us wanted to leave Kert behind to his fate, but we couldn't think of a way to free him.

"Perhaps we should consider fire," Ambrose suggested after a moment. "Build one at the base of the trunk, or burn the offending limb."

I shook my head. "A fire that close to the tree is just going to harm him, too."

"The man has taken enough damage already," Trut agreed. "Even if we free him, that hand of his is ruined. He'll never use it properly again. There's no sense burning him on top of that."

"So," I replied, "we've got two choices. We can leave him here to his fate, or we can amputate his hand and free him. I won't go for the first, and I'll go against anyone who chooses it. But I don't care for the second choice, either."

"It's not so bad." Trut patted his stump. "You get used to it after a while. You adapt. And besides, Kert will still have the rest of his arm. He ought to consider himself lucky."

"I have seen the toll dismemberment wreaks on young men," Ambrose told him. "Such injuries are one of the most detestable sureties of war. I do not think this Kert will share your outlook after we lop off his hand."

"Even if we do this," Marta said, "he will still not be able to travel or fight. If we abandon him here in that state, is it not the same as leaving him attached to the tree?"

"Will any of you volunteer to stay with him?" I glanced around at them. "I hate to ask, but there's no other way. Somebody needs to stay behind and watch over him. When he's well enough to travel, you'll have to guide him back to the village."

They all looked at each other. Then Sleeth stepped forward. She looked nervous.

"I will do it," she said. "Kert is ... was ... a friend of my father. I had hoped to avenge my father today, but doing this will honor him, too."

"Your father died in the attack on the village?" I asked.

"I do not know," the girl answered. "He was wounded when we left, but still alive. I hope that he will be waiting for me when I return."

I was hesitant to leave Sleeth behind by herself, and not out of any sort of misguided chivalry or sexism. Most of the women in the tribe were as capable—or even more capable—than the men. Indeed, Kasheena had saved my life more times than I could count. But Sleeth was not a warrior. She was a young girl, frail and slender and possessing an innocence and naivety that suggested this was her first time venturing away from the boundaries of the village.

"Do you think you can find your way back to the village on your own?" I asked her.

Sleeth hesitated, before stammering, "I ... I do not know. If I follow the marks on the trees that our trackers have left behind ...?"

She was brave, for sure, but she also doubted herself, and while I admired her courage, I was troubled by the repercussions that uncertainty could create should they run into trouble. How would she fare up against a dinosaur or a giant robot or any of the other dangers the Lost Level presented? Kert would be unable to fight, given his condition, and as much as I hated to admit it, Sleeth wouldn't fare well in combat on her own. Yes, she was a deadly shot with her sling and stones, but a weapon like that would do little good against giants like an allosaurus or a Tyrannosaurus Rex, or even smaller opponents like the amorphous, carnivorous blobs that roamed the land.

"I know the way home," Martek said, stepping forward. "I will go with her, Aaron, if you will permit me?"

His gaze darted nervously to Sleeth and then back to me. Martek's ears turned red. The hue matched the color blooming on Sleeth's pale cheeks. I struggled to suppress a smile. My thoughts turned to Kasheena. Obviously, Martek had feelings for Sleeth. I put myself in his shoes. What if I were traipsing through the woods with a war party and the woman I loved was tasked with staying behind? I would want to stay at her side.

I realized that, with the exception of Martek and Sleeth, the rest of the group was looking at me, waiting for a response. The two teenagers kept their eyes on their feet, and judging by how stiffly they stood, both seemed to be holding their breath.

"Very well," I said. "Both of you will stay with Kert until he is well enough to travel. Then I want you to head for the village, and tell the others what has happened so far. If there are others among our people who are well enough to travel, I want you to guide them back here. We'll continue blazing the trail. Follow along after us. By the time you find us, we may need reinforcements. Fair enough?"

Both of them nodded, exhaling with obvious relief. The rest of the group seemed okay with the decision. Only Flik showed any sign of distress. He didn't speak, but his eyes remained focused on Martek, and it was clear to me that he felt saddened and afraid.

"Flik," I said, "I want you to take over for Kert."

He jerked in surprise. "I am not a tracker, Aaron."

"Maybe not, but you're going to learn to be. I want you to stick by Tolia's side. She moves fast. You'll need to keep up."

He nodded, swallowing hard. It was my hope that by giving him this new task, I would alleviate some of his sadness over being split up from his friends.

Martek stepped forward and held out my sword. "Here, Aaron. It was an honor to carry it."

"You keep it," I told him. "We both know you're going to need it before you get home. I'll get it back from you when we return. Deal?"

I stuck out my hand and smiled. Grinning, Martek shook my hand.

"Deal," he replied.

"Okay," I ordered. "Somebody get a fire going. We'll need to cauterize the wound. Karenk, you're the strongest among us. Think you can do this?"

The big man's expression turned queasy, but he drew his sword with confidence. "I will do what needs to be done, Aaron. Kert would do the same for me."

We did our best to keep Kert distracted while we waited for the fire. In truth, the tree did most of our work for us. Although he must have been aware of our preparations, Kert seemed untroubled by the activity taking place around him. I noticed with horror that his blood had vanished from the tree branch, having been sucked into the wood itself. Worse, the skin on his hand—already torn and ruptured from our attempt to free him—

was starting to dissolve. It gave off a faint, acrid stench that reminded me of a ruptured car battery.

Soon, Marta stepped forward with a blazing torch. Her hand trembled as she held it aloft. I nodded at Karenk, and he moved to Kert's side. His jaw was set, his shoulders stiff.

"Karune, Tolia, and Tomkin," I said. "Help me hold him."

Karune and Tomkin grabbed Kert's legs. Tolia kept hold of his free arm. I grabbed his other arm, just below his shoulder.

"The tree doesn't like this," Kert murmured. His words were slurred and drool dribbled from the corner of his mouth. "It won't let me go! I don't want to go ..."

"Shhhh," I soothed. "Just hang on, buddy. It will all be over with soon."

"But, Aaron ..."

"I'm sorry, Kert. I really am. Just stay with us."

Kert started to respond, but Karenk suddenly raised the sword with both hands and brought it whistling down in a mighty arc. His aim was true. The strike hit just above Kert's wrist. I winced at the sound the blade made as it cleaved through his flesh. Blood splattered my face, arms, and chest. I turned away, grimacing as drops of it ran into my eyes and mouth. Blinking it away, I spat to the side.

Kert began to thrash and scream. It felt like we were holding a live electric wire. Despite the fact that there were four of us, it took all of our strength to keep a grip on him.

"Keep hold," Tolia shouted.

"The bone," Karenk groaned.

I turned to look. The sword had sliced through the flesh and splintered Kert's wrist bone, but hadn't severed his hand all the way. His arm was still attached by veins and tendons and a flap of skin. Kert jerked violently in our grip, whipping his head back and forth. He tried to bite Tolia, but she elbowed him in the face. Cursing, Karenk quickly sawed the sword back and forth, slicing through the remaining gristle and finishing the job. Kert immediately slumped backward, blood spraying in an arc from his stump. His amputated hand remained stuck to the tree.

"Torch," I shouted, but Marta was already moving. She thrust the blazing brand at Kert's flailing arm, and we forced his wrist into the flame. Kert's anguished screams turned into one long, mournful wail, and then he mercifully passed out. The flame popped and hissed as Kert's blood and body fat sizzled. My stomach roiled at the smell of burning flesh, but I gritted my teeth and held him firm, until I was certain that the fire had cauterized the wound.

"Okay," I gasped. "That's enough. Lay him down."

I inspected the charred, reeking stump. It was black and pink and oozing, but ultimately, I was satisfied that the torch had done its job. While Kert was still unconscious, we bound the wound, using some scraps of cloth and the leather straps from my sling. Then I gazed up at the others.

"Do we have anything to give him for the pain?"

They shook their heads. Then, Tomkin shyly raised one hand.

"I brought along a wineskin," he admitted. "But it's nearly empty now."

"Give it to Martek and Sleeth," I said. "Anything will help."

"I'm just happy to hear that there is wine to be found in this abominable place," Ambrose quipped.

I climbed to my feet and glanced around. I couldn't help but notice the severed hand, still stuck to the tree. Was it my imagination, or did it seem smaller now? Perhaps the tree, realizing this morsel was all it would get to eat that day, was consuming it more rapidly. The idea made me queasy—but also angry.

"Marta?" I nodded at the still-blazing torch in her hand, and then pointed at the tree. "No sense in letting that fire go to waste."

"I wouldn't," Trut cautioned. "If we're near the Anunnaki, they might see the smoke."

"We would also have to wait and keep the fire from spreading," Tolia advised. "We are gaining ground on the snake men. Another delay would cost us."

I sighed. "Point taken."

Marta extinguished the torch and the campfire, while the others knelt beside Kert, watching over him in concern. Only Tolia, Karenk, and Fern stood apart from the group. Fern had found a purple-winged butterfly to play with, and Tolia was staring into the ravine, clearly anxious to get back on the trail. Karenk stood some distance away, hunched over in the underbrush. His shoulders heaved, and I heard him retching. When he rejoined us, wiping his mouth with the back of his hand, his complexion was pale.

"Are you going to be okay?" I asked.

He nodded. "I will be fine. These things have never bothered me before, but this is the first time I have...had to strike against a fellow member of our tribe. I do not like the feeling it leaves behind."

Ambrose moved to him then and placed a hand on Karenk's broad shoulder. He spoke softly, and I couldn't catch the words, but whatever his counsel, the barbarian seemed to relax.

I took Martek and Sleeth aside and handed Sleeth the small pouch of round stones that had served as ammunition for my sling, since I wouldn't be needing them anymore. Then I instructed the two of them to wait by Kert's side, giving him water and aid, until he had sufficiently recovered. When they judged he was able to travel, I told them to make the journey back to the village. If there were any able-bodied fighters left, Martek was to bring them back as reinforcements and follow our trail.

"What if Kert does not recover?" he asked. "What if he dies?"

"Then you and Sleeth will have to decide what to do. You

can come after us, or take his body back to the village so that his family can bury him. I'll leave that decision up to you."

It occurred to me that there was a very good chance Kert might, in fact, succumb to his wound. Although the fire had done its job, he was lying on the forest floor—a far cry from the sanitary conditions of a hospital or operating room. His hand had been amputated with a sword, rather than a sterilized scalpel or saw—a sword that, only a day before, had lopped the heads and arms off Anunnaki. I knew that Karenk prided himself in the care of his blade, and that he had cleaned it after the battle, but I doubted the sword had been disinfected.

"Do what you can," I told them quietly, so that the rest of the group wouldn't overhear. "Keep him comfortable and dry. We've lost too many already ..."

Martek nodded.

"We will," Sleeth whispered.

"But if he is ... suffering ... if it looks like his wound will kill him, then you'll have another decision to make. I'm leaving that in your hands, as well. Do you understand?"

This time, they both nodded.

Tolia headed down into the ravine and scouted the ground until she found tracks. Then, without a word, she headed out. Flik rushed to keep up with her. The young man glanced back once and waved at Martek and Sleeth. His expression was sad—and fearful. It mirrored their own expressions. The rest of us followed along behind. This time, I brought up the rear of the procession.

When I looked back, Martek and Sleeth's hands were still raised, waving farewell. I returned the gesture, and then the greenery closed over them, and they disappeared from my sight, as if the forest had swallowed them both.

# [ 7 ]
# DEATH STALKS THE STONE PLAIN

We followed the ravine for a long time, finding an occasional bit of interdimensional flotsam and jetsam among the rocks and dirt—a broken shard of blue bottle glass, a weathered and frayed length of rope, the splintered remains of a wooden pallet, a decapitated doll's head with one missing eye, some rusty bent nails, a plastic soft drink bottle, a scrap of twisted metal, a crumpled and empty pack of Turkish cigarettes, a plastic fork that had melted and warped in the sun, and other equally useless items. The tribe members paid them only a cursory glance, and I had been here long enough to grow accustomed to finding things like these. Only Ambrose was curious about them, and even then, his interest lay more in how they had ended up here than what they actually were. Judging by the condition of the ground, and the height of the vegetation around us, the ravine had been dry for a very long time, so it was doubtful they'd been washed and deposited there by a flood.

Eventually, the Anunnaki's trail exited the ravine and led back up into the forest. We followed it, using the jutting, dangling roots of the trees above the gulch to scale the treacherous embankment. At the top, we discovered a discarded piece of clothing from one of the captives, snagged on a thorny thicket. We couldn't be sure of the owner, but we were certain it was from our tribe. That find seemed to spur us on even faster. I kept peering ahead into the woods, expecting to see Kasheena and the others appear at any moment. When they didn't, my spirits sank. I idly checked my .45, opening the cylinder and making sure the revolver was fully loaded. I already knew that it was, of course, but I was desperate for something—anything—to take my mind off the plight of Kasheena and the other prisoners.

"That's an interesting weapon," Ambrose remarked. "Obviously, it looks somewhat different than what I am accustomed to, and yet it is instantly recognizable. A forty-five caliber, if I had to guess?"

"You're right. That's a pretty impressive guess, Mister Bierce."

"Please, Aaron. Call me Ambrose. And as I said, I know guns. They haven't changed too much, even in your time. There is a comforting familiarity in that. May I examine it?"

He held out his hand. I snapped the cylinder shut and gave him the pistol. I didn't bother to unload it or caution him on the proper way to handle it. A veteran like Ambrose Bierce would certainly know how to handle a gun, even one that was manufactured long after his supposed death. He studied it with appreciation, holding it, balancing it, gauging its weight, and sighting through it, before finally handing it back to me.

"I don't suppose you have a spare that I could arm myself with?"

"I wish," I replied, "but sadly, no. Although, if we come across a shotgun, I've got some spare twelve gauge shells on me that you can use for it."

"I will do my best to find one, then. Does that happen frequently—finding discarded weaponry?"

I told him about the things I'd found since coming here, including the weapons that were from beyond my time—or from worlds other than our own: laser rifles and heat rays and guns that were so advanced I'd never been able to determine their purpose. I talked about the crashed Nazi Bell flying craft I'd discovered in a field, and the dangers it had presented, which then led to a discussion of the state of Germany from the time he'd departed his timeline, and what they had turned into during the First and Second World Wars. Ambrose was eager to hear more about Earth's future history, and I told him what I could of the two World Wars and the invention of the atomic bomb, as well as the so-called Cold War, and the wars in Korea, Vietnam, the Persian Gulf, Desert Storm, and the post 9/11 wars in Iraq and Afghanistan. That led me to wonder if they were still ongoing back home. Had those problems been solved? Was religious extremism and colonial nationalism still a thing? It was strange to think that anything could be happening back on Earth—another war, another massive-scaled terrorist attack, or maybe a peace accord—and I had no knowledge of it here. The thought made me sad, and for the first time in a long while, I felt a pang of homesickness.

Ambrose sighed. "It truly never ends. We like to think that men of the future will find a way to live in peace, but they don't. Take this weapon you mentioned—this harnessing of nuclear energy. Men invented that destructive weapon with the expectation of it bringing about some universal peace, but instead, they merely ushered in new implements of war. They were no wiser than a farmer who, noticing the improvement of agricultural implements, predicts an end to the tilling of the soil."

"Oh, farming has changed, too," I told him. "In my time—"

Ambrose held up his hand, cutting me off. "No, do not tell me. I dread hearing about it. I can only imagine their plight where you come from."

"There's not many of them left," I admitted. "Most of the farms are run by giant corporations now. There are a lot of concerns about the quality of our food and what we might be ingesting."

"And yet," Ambrose said, "the American people allow this to happen. They are sheep in my time, and judging by the sound, they remain sheep in yours. And so, there's a new war every decade or so, the purpose of which seems to be to teach them geography, and they blindly support it in the name of patriotism. Bleating sheep."

"They still love to wave the flag," I agreed. "They complain that there's nobody worth voting for, but they line up to vote every four years, regardless. All in the name of patriotism."

"Do you know what patriotism really is, Aaron?"

"Loving your country?"

"Hogwash." Ambrose spat on the ground. "Patriotism is nothing more than combustible rubbish, ready for the torch of any politician wishing to make a name for himself. That is one of the things I find most alluring about this new world that I suddenly find myself in. The people of this tribe may be more primitive, but they are also free of all the baggage that comes with our civilization. Just the fact that there are no politicians or nationalism in this place is enough to interest me."

"Well, there aren't any politicians among these people, at least," I reminded him, "but the Lost Level is a big place, Mr. Bierce. It's possible those things do exist here. War certainly does. We're marching off to war right now. Some of us have died already, and I'm sure more of us will before we are through."

"But it is a just war—a noble war, if such a thing can be considered noble. You are doing this not because some bloated bag of wind is encouraging you for God or country, but simply to save your loved ones. Yes, you will shed blood. You will murder. But you will do so for a cause that is right. There are four kinds of homicide, Aaron—felonious, excusable, justifiable, and praiseworthy. I believe that any of these snake men that you gun down in the process of saving your beloved can count as excusable and justifiable. And, if you make a particularly difficult shot with that revolver, then perhaps it will count as praiseworthy, too."

He winked at me and chuckled to himself, which then led to a bout of coughing and wheezing. Fern glanced up at him, and I swear I saw concern in the baby dinosaur's eyes.

"I am fine," Ambrose said, cutting off my query before I could even ask. "Now come along. We are falling behind, and I strongly suspect that Tolia will not wait for us."

"No," I agreed. "She definitely won't."

As the forest began to thin even more, the vegetation and undergrowth grew thicker. Soon, we were hacking our way through thorns and vines—only a few of which fought back. I saw signs that other beings, in addition to the Anunnaki, had passed through the area, as well. There were places where the greenery was slashed or flattened, and numerous narrow game trails leading in all different directions. I was amazed by Tolia's tracking abilities. She paused occasionally, getting her bearings, but not once did she lead us astray or have to backtrack. Somehow, she was able to determine the Anunnaki's path from that of a herd of deer, and divine where the snake men had laid down instead of a spot where a dinosaur had bedded.

We came upon a thicket of purple thorns, which several of our party recognized. After Tolia warned the rest of us that they were poisonous and "would make our blood boil like acid in our veins," we decided to go around. Apparently, the Anunnaki had done the same thing, because we quickly reconnected with their trail, once we'd rounded and cleared the thicket.

"I'm taking that as a good sign," I told the others.

"What?" Flik asked.

"That the snake men took the time to go around those poisonous thorns, rather than force our people to hack their way through them. It means they are doing their best to keep their captives alive until they reach their final destination."

"But why?" Tomkin asked.

"I don't know," I admitted. "They need them for something, obviously. I can't imagine that it's for anything good, though."

Tolia started forward again. "That is why we must make certain we catch up to them before they reach their destination."

Soon after, the trees grew so sparse that we were no longer in the forest at all, and instead found ourselves emerging onto a grassy plain, much like the one we'd started on. The only difference was that this part of the landscape was much shorter by comparison. The grass and wildflowers soon ended, and the dirt was replaced with massive slabs of rock and boulders. Indeed, as we pressed on, I was stunned by the absolute lack of vegetation or greenery. We stood amidst a plain of stone. The only things growing here were the moss and lichen that clung to the rocks and an occasional stunted, spindly and leafless tree jutting from between the boulders. Nothing moved, save the wind, moaning as it winnowed across the rocks.

"I have seen some desolate places in my time," Ambrose muttered, "but this one beats all."

The stone plain stretched out all around us, and I could see no end in sight. The horizon was filled with more barren emptiness. In the far distance, I spied some jagged spires and crags where the rocks rose even higher, but there were no buildings or forests or anything else of note.

Finally, Tolia paused, dropping to one knee and examining the stones beneath our feet. Frowning, she stared at the ground for a long time. Then she stood up and walked to another spot, where she repeated the same action. The rest of us waited while she did this a few more times. When she stood again, her expression was troubled.

"Have you lost their trail?" I asked.

Tolia shook her head. "I can still follow them, but we will have to move more slowly. They are tough to track among these rocks, and they will move faster, now that they don't have the vegetation to impede them. The good news is that we are catching up to them. If we keep a fast pace, we can overtake them before our next rest. Those marks are fresh. They passed this way not long ago."

She pointed at a large stone slab. I followed the gesture but saw no marks or scratches or other signs of passage.

"I'll take your word for it. If we're that close, we should try to stay as quiet as possible. Everybody check your gear. Make sure your weapons are muffled and your canteens aren't rattling. We don't want them to hear our swords banging against our legs or scraping against a boulder."

Nodding and murmuring among themselves, the group began to do as I'd told them.

"How is everyone fixed for water?" I asked. "From the looks of things, it might be a while before we find some again. This area looks pretty inhospitable."

"It does," Karenk agreed, "but we have to assume the snake men have passed through this way before. They need water, too. There must be resources at some point."

I nodded. "Probably so. But just to be safe, let's be careful with our food and water. Trut, have you ever been through here?"

"Once," he replied, "when I was much younger and still had both my eyes. But we only skirted the edges of this barren plain, sticking to the grasslands. If I remember correctly, there is a vast desert on the other side—a place even more desolate than this region. I don't know what lies beyond that, but it seems to me it would be suicide for us to cross it."

"In your opinion, do you think that's where the Anunnaki are heading? To the desert?"

Trut frowned, thinking. Then, after a moment he shook his head.

"The desert would be sunny enough for them. That is certain. They need sunlight and warmth. But as Karenk said, they also need water, just like all other living things do. No, I suspect that we are close to their lair. I would guess that it's somewhere among these stones. If we—"

He never got to finish because at that moment a shadow passed over us, darkening the ground. One by one, we all glanced upward too late as a massive pterodactyl plunged shrieking out of the sky, seized Tomkin in its talons, and yanked him off the ground. I don't know where it came from. Perhaps it had watched us from the treetops in the forest, or maybe it had perched on one of the higher stone spires or boulders. Wherever it had hidden, the monster's approach had been silent and quick. It hadn't cried out until it was upon us, a tactic it had adopted to scare its prey into pausing. Still, despite the rapidity of its attack, the creature's escape took much longer. Tomkin was a beefy mountain of a man, and the pterodactyl had difficulty taking off with him. He balled both fists and struck the talons, but to no avail. The beast croaked loudly, sounding like a rusty hinge, and struggled to take flight again. It rose, and then fell, but didn't dislodge its prey. Tomkin kicked wildly, his feet skimming the stones a few times, but then the creature righted itself and soared skyward, grunting. Tomkin shrieked, still beating helplessly at it with his fists. His cries grew fainter as the monster flew higher.

Before I could even shout the order, Tolia and our other archers had their bows out, aiming at the dinosaur's wings. I followed suit with my pistol, pausing only long enough to space my feet apart at shoulder-width. Holding it with both hands, I raised the .45, extending my arms and locking my elbows. Holding my breath, I drew a bead on the target. My heart sank. Already, it was almost out of range. I was just about to take the shot anyway, when somebody screamed behind me. A sudden gust of wind ruffled my hair. Before I could turn, a searing pain ripped through my back and shoulders. The pressure on my body was immense, as if I'd been trapped in a vise. Seconds later, I, too, was yanked off the ground.

At first, I didn't understand what was happening to me. The pain was too intense, and I think I must have blacked out for a second. When I became aware again, my skin felt hot and flushed and my ears were ringing. I had trouble focusing my vision. Everything seemed to tilt and blur. I kicked my feet back and forth in the air, watching the terrified expressions of the rest of my party far below. Some of them were shouting, but I couldn't understand the words. I squeezed the pistol's handle tightly, seeking comfort from its familiarity. The ringing in my ears grew louder, and the pressure on my shoulders was immense. I glanced down at my chest and saw my blood dripping away like rain rolling off a car's windshield. It was then that I finally began to come to my senses, and—realizing what was happening—I screamed.

Like Tomkin, I'd been seized and plucked from the ground by a pterodactyl.

I shrieked again, and the predator answered me with a cry of its own. I swear to you, it sounded like the thing was laughing. When I glanced down again, the others were far, far below. We were already high enough that I could no longer discern their faces. A few arrows arced toward us, but all of them fell short. I watched them fall away like toothpicks.

The pterodactyl croaked again, flapping its leathery wings, and readjusted its grip on me. The pain and pressure on my shoulders grew worse as the creature's talons dug deeper into the meat of my back and chest, squeezing me. The pressure from those talons would have been immobilizing if not for my resolve. But even my will was no match for my opponent. I was as helpless as a rabbit in the clutches of a horned owl. I struggled just to stay conscious. The agony was so intense, so incapacitating, that I couldn't even raise my arms. Indeed, it took everything I had just to hold on to my pistol. But even if I had been able to shoot the monster at this height, such an action would have proven fatal for us both. Even in the depths of shock, I had enough presence of mind to realize that much.

All I could do was watch helplessly, dangling in the thing's clutches, battling to keep my wits about me as we soared over the stone plain. I gaped in panicked bewilderment, my sense of direction lost as the landscape rushed by below us. Everything looked the same to me—a vast, inhospitable, windswept wasteland of rocks and boulders, canyons and fissures, natural spires and craggy cavern mouths. There was no greenery or water—only hard stone.

Occasionally, I glimpsed Tomkin, still struggling in the grip of the other pterodactyl. I wondered dimly if we would die together. I wished idly that I'd taken the time to know him better.

The dinosaur smelled revolting, and each time the creature beat its massive wings, I recoiled from the wafting stink that enveloped me. My stomach churned. When I breathed, I could taste the stench at the back of my throat. It reminded me of two distinctly unpleasant smells from my youth. The first was during a family trip to a zoo in Minneapolis, and the particular odor that had seemed to permeate the reptile house—a smell not unlike that of the Anunnaki. The second was even more revolting. When I was a kid, a friend of mine's parents owned a turkey farm. The place always stank of feathers and shit, especially in the summer, when the heat seemed to transform it into an almost physical thing. The stench used to waft off the farm, blown by the breeze, and we could smell it from miles away if the wind was right. It seemed to me now that someone had opened up a reptile house in the middle of a turkey farm and then dropped me into it.

My stomach continued to churn until I couldn't take it any longer. I retched, choked, and managed to lean forward before I puked. My vomit streamed behind us, raining to the ground along with my blood. The pterodactyl croaked again.

"Fuck you, too," I gasped. My throat felt raw.

All the while, the motionless sun beat down upon us, making the entire experience even more miserable. The brightness gave me a headache, and the throbbing in my temples seemed to act in conjunction with the agony in my shoulders. My pistol grew heavy, and I struggled to keep my grip on it. My arms began to tremble, and soon, my whole body was shaking. Despite the baking heat, I felt cold—either from blood loss, shock, or a change in atmospheric pressure.

Or possibly all three.

We climbed higher and higher, and I began to get dizzy. My stomach roiled again, my anus puckered, and it felt like my testicles were shrinking up inside of me. I had to close my eyes against the vertigo, and even then, the sensation remained overpowering. Back on my own world, I had never cared much for flying. It had always seemed unnatural to me to sit inside a metal tube and get launched into the air at incredible speeds and heights, with no control over your own safety or directional course—but at that moment, I would have gladly welcomed an airplane. Even more, I would have welcomed the three or four Bloody Marys I used to down at airport bars before boarding my flight. They had always helped me cope with my fears before, and I could have used a vat of them as we soared on.

The air began to grow cooler as we flew higher still. When my ears popped from the change in air pressure, I started to cry. Not for Kasheena and the rest of the captives. I was confident that, despite our rescue mission, Kasheena would survive if able. She'd mount an escape or a defense. And I didn't cry for the remaining members of the rescue party. They were in good hands. Tolia or Karenk or perhaps Trut could lead them just as well as I had—possibly even better. No, who I cried for was myself. I cried because I wanted to see Kasheena again. I cried because I was utterly terrified. I had known fear since coming to the Lost Level. You don't stare down a voracious allosaurus or fight a giant killer robot or hide from flying piranha and not be scared while doing those things. But that type of fear is a motivator—it drives you. Fuels you. That type of fear prods you into action, and it isn't until the danger is over that you stop and consider how perilous it actually was. It isn't until then that you truly realize that you could have died.

This situation was far different than any of those. I dangled helplessly in the clutches of this giant prehistoric bird, unable to shoot, stab, punch, slice, talk, or think my way out of it. Death—an agonizing death—seemed a certainty, and the sureness and nearness of it, and the fact that no matter how strong my will, I couldn't cheat it, fueled my despair. Heavy as I felt at that moment, had the pterodactyl released me, I would have dropped much faster than any stone.

Very dimly, I thought I heard Tomkin crying as well, though that might have been my imagination—or perhaps just the echoes of my own sobs, blown back to me on the wind. When I opened my eyes to see if I could spy him, I saw something else instead.

There, far below, was a vast depression of some kind—a natural bowl carved into the rocky plain. It might have been half a mile deep and a similar length across, though it was hard to gauge for certain from that height. What interested me more than its size were the structures I spotted within the depths of the basin—tall, spiraling stone towers and sprawling buildings made of brick and rock. All of them had been built, rather than having formed naturally, and from what I glimpsed, the masonry and craftsmanship were of a very high quality. There was a large courtyard, roughly the size of a football field, and the edges of it were dotted with dome-shaped structures. A cluster of mud huts stood off to one side. Curiously, in the center of the courtyard, I spotted what appeared to be a great pit, but it was impossible to see into its blackened depths. All around the edges of the city, where the walls of the bowl sloped upward to rejoin the rest of the stone plain, were hundreds of cave mouths. The city bustled with activity, but the height made the figures appear as nothing more than ants, and the vertigo returned. I closed my eyes again and shuddered.

Dangling from the pterodactyl's claws, blind and close to unconsciousness, I pondered what I had just seen, and wondered if it could have been the Anunnaki's final destination. Their city, perhaps? It was hard to be sure, undefinable as the figures I'd seen scurrying around had been. If they were the snake men, then their numbers were far greater than we had ever dared to imagine, given the number of figures I'd seen swarming about.

When I sensed that we had finally leveled out again, I risked opening my eyes. There was no sign of the city I'd glimpsed before. Instead, ahead of us rose a mountain peak formed of jagged, twisting stone spires. The pterodactyls bore us steadily toward it, seeming to increase their speed. The dread built inside of me again, threatening to explode.

"Tomkin!" I tried to shout, but the wind ripped my voice away.

The pterodactyl flexed its talons, and instead of shouting, I screamed.

Up we soared, circling the natural stone spires. A new sound suggested itself to me, borne on the wind—the incessant squawking of a multitude of tiny voices. I opened my eyes wider and spotted tree trunks and other debris jumbled below, scattered across a broad plateau centered between the spires and over-looking the plain. At first, I couldn't figure out what I was looking at, but then we began a circling descent and it all became clearer.

The debris formed two giant, sprawling nests. As we swooped lower, I saw dozens of pterodactyl hatchlings gawking up at us, cawing with anticipation. My captor croaked a response. The cry echoed across the rocks. The babies craned their necks higher, snapping their beaks hungrily, and flapping about in the nests, tromping over discarded egg shells, piles of feces, bones, and tree branches.

The other adult pterodactyl loomed in my sight again for a brief moment, just long enough for me to see it drop Tomkin into one of the nests from a height of around ten feet. He fell like a rag doll, limp and seemingly lifeless. Amazingly, the dinosaur's aim had deposited him in a portion of the nest where there were no eggs or babies. Having done so, the pterodactyl swooped skyward again.

Then it was my turn. The nest loomed, filling my vision. I drew a breath to shout, but before I could, the pressure on my shoulders decreased, bringing a fresh rout of pain as the dinosaur released me. The talons ripped free of my flesh, further gouging my wounds. I convulsed in agony, and my pistol slipped from my grasp.

As I plummeted toward the hungry hordes below, the wind seemed to roar in my ears. The pain vanished, replaced by a creeping coldness that numbed both my body and mind. I caught a glimpse of my .45 tumbling away, flashing in the sunlight. Then it struck the rocks and disappeared. A second later, I crashed into the nest, and the pain returned tenfold. Scratched and battered by dozens of broken branches, I lay there on my back, struggling just to breathe. A shadow passed over me as my former captor flew overhead. Then, the beast whirled up into the sky again and headed back out over the plain.

The incessant cries of the baby pterodactyls grew shriller and more incensed. There was an immediacy to their squabbling, a primal urgency that was as bone-chilling and harrowing as the sounds their adult counterparts had made. Once again, despite my panic and fear, I found myself marveling over the dinosaur's aim. It had managed to drop me unerringly into the center of the nest—a bare area with no eggs or hatchlings.

Groaning, I tried to move my legs and arms. Doing so was an exercise in agony, and that pain got even worse as something sliced into my thigh. I glanced down and saw a furious newborn, not much bigger than a good-sized crow, jabbing at my leg with its beak—the tip of which was red.

Something snapped inside me upon seeing my own blood. My strength and wits returned, and the pain seemed to recede. My body felt as if it were on fire. I kicked the diminutive creature aside, sending it tottering backward. The other babies crawled toward me, plodding along unsteadily on newborn feet and dragging themselves along with their stunted wings. Another one snapped at my ear, but I rolled to the side and lashed out with my fist, pulping the infant in mid-squawk. The webbed skin felt strangely hot beneath my own flesh. When I raised my hand, blood and yellow innards dripped from my fingers. I flung a handful of gore at another approaching chick and then sprang to my feet. I stomped around the nest, crushing eggs and birds beneath the soles of my leather boots, snapping bones and tree branches alike. The nest rustled with activity as the frenzied spawn swarmed in all directions—some fleeing and others lurching forward to attack. I kicked away any that got too close, while desperately glancing around, searching for a means of escape. A glint of sunlight reflecting off metal caught my eye, and I made my way toward it. I grabbed hold of a sturdy branch, and wrenched it free of the compacted nest. Doing so brought my pain back into focus again, but I ignored it and pushed ahead, swinging the club back and forth, clearing a path. Sure enough, the shiny object turned out to be my fallen pistol. I reached down, swept it up, and drew a bead on the closest bird. After a second, I considered my actions and thought better of it. It was pointless to waste ammunition on such small targets when my makeshift club would suffice. I was running on shock and panic. What I needed to do was tamp down both and find a way out of this situation.

Ahead of me, a thick cluster of young pterodactyls busied themselves with what remained of Tomkin—and it wasn't much. In the short time since we'd been deposited here, the hatchlings had stripped the flesh and eyes from his face, as well as most of the skin on his neck, arms and legs. My throat burned as I choked down bile. I was just about to turn away when Tomkin moved. His left hand twitched, and his arm started to rise.

"Oh shit," I moaned. "You're still alive. Hang on, Tomkin! I'm ..."

Then I realized that the movements were caused by the birds pecking away at him. My gorge rose again. Holstering my pistol, I wheeled around and charged toward the edge of the nest, mindlessly crushing anything in my path. When I reached the side, I quickly peered over it and saw a ledge about four feet wide, circling the plateau. Beyond that was a dizzying drop down to the plain far below. Remarkably, the cliff face seemed to curve inward, and I couldn't make out any means of descent.

I bit my lip, staring at the gulf. Then, a hatchling lashed at the back of my ankle, drawing fresh blood, and I resolved to try it. Better to die plunging over that cliff than to be pecked to death here in this forsaken, filthy nest. I vaulted over the side, landed on both feet, and steadied myself. Then, ignoring every impulse to run, I inched along the ledge and slowly made my way along the lip.

A shadow passed over me again. It was followed by a deep, echoing croak.

I glanced up. The adult pterodactyls had returned, enraged over the damage I'd caused inside the nest. Both of them zoomed toward me, blotting out the sun. They shrieked in unison, and then one made a sort of throaty hissing noise, the way a mother duck will do when protecting her young. The sound reverberated off the boulders.

I flung myself off the ledge, feeling the pressure of their wings behind me, hearing their talons scrape against the rock where I'd been standing just a second before.

Then I was falling so fast that not even the pterodactyls could keep up with me.

# [ 8 ]
## THE TUNNEL

I spun, plummeting downward, catching pin-wheeling glimpses of brown and gray rocks and blue sky—a bewildering, spiraling kaleidoscope of shifting colors and textures and surfaces. The angry shrieks of my pursuers faded. The only sound was the wind roaring in my ears, drowning out everything else, even my screams. As terrifying as my capture and ascent in the clutches of the pterodactyl had been, this was somehow worse. Even while in the dinosaur's claws, I'd still had hope. I'd still had the will to fight, if an opportunity presented itself—and it had. But there was no way to fight against the pull of gravity. It wasn't a foe you could outwit or outrace. You couldn't stab it or shoot it. The only thing you could do was surrender to its unrelenting force. Gravity always won in the end. The only mercy in it was that my descent would be much faster than my flight had been, and given the rate of speed I was falling, with any luck I'd be rendered unconscious before I struck the bottom.

You can imagine my surprise, then, when neither of those things happened. Instead of passing out, I became aware that the terrain had changed. I could no longer see the sky, but that's about all I understood of this new predicament. I had a vague sense of tumbling through some sort of enclosed space. And instead of landing with an explosive splat at the bottom of the cliff, I careened against more rocks and stone. My ears rang. My vision went black. I pinged around like a pinball, caroming off structures I couldn't see. Now, instead of free-falling, I rolled head over heels, battered against a hard surface, adding fresh pain to my already serious injuries. I tucked myself into a ball as best I could, trying to minimize any further damage. The agony was so overwhelming that I briefly forgot all about Kasheena and everyone else who needed my help. I wished instead for oblivion, if only to escape the pain, but stubborn consciousness persisted. It wasn't until I smashed against a boulder and came to a sudden, jarring stop that I was finally blessed with what I'd craved.

I don't know how long I lay there, but when I regained consciousness, I found myself exposed to one of the Lost Level's rarest things—darkness. Well, okay. Maybe not a total darkness. But for the first time since I'd left the village and set out on this rescue mission, I couldn't sense the sun overhead. Even in the depths of the forest, we'd known it was there, lurking above the treetops. But not now. The sun's warmth was gone, and what little light I could see was filtered, as if coming to me from a great distance. I lay there shivering, but I wasn't sure if it was from shock or cold. It was hard to breathe. When I tried to move, the pain was so excruciating that I passed out again.

The next time I opened my eyes, nothing had changed. I was still in shadows, still trembling, and still in pain. Instead of moving, I decided just to stay very still for a while and let my senses recover. I was still having difficulty breathing, especially through my nose. Then I lost consciousness a third time.

When I came to once more, the first thing I became aware of was that I was lying on my back, on what felt like stone. I sensed no dampness or moisture, but the surface was cool enough to explain why I felt cold—at least, I hoped. It occurred to me that I might be in a cave of some sort. I listened intently for the sound of dripping water, but all I heard were the very distant cries of the frustrated pterodactyls. They seemed muffled, and their source was odd—echoing from above me but to the right, as if the sound waves were coming from around a curve.

Eventually, I experimented with moving, starting with my feet. The soles of my boots were covered in baby pterodactyl blood and tiny twigs. I wiggled my toes and discovered that they still worked. Then I tried raising my legs one at a time. I clenched my teeth, hissing at the pain this caused. It wasn't the sharp, urgent agony that accompanies a broken bone, but it hurt all the same. Still, at least I wasn't paralyzed. Moving on to my arms, I tried lifting each of them. Surprisingly, they stuck to the stone floor as if glued there. I pulled harder, yanking them free. Both arms were covered in blood. Some of it had dried to a rusty brown color, but overtop that layer was bright red, which meant I was still bleeding. I lowered my arms and then shifted my weight back and forth, working my body from side to side. My bloodied back and shoulders also stuck to the floor, and I winced as they tore free. I closed my eyes until the pain subsided, and then I tried raising my head. Doing so brought about the worst pain yet, but I forced myself to sit up. The blood had matted my hair, and some of it tore free at the roots, but I pushed on. When I was finally upright, I sat there, panting. It was still hard to breathe through my nose. I soon discovered that this was because both nostrils were clogged with blood. I cleared my nose, blowing red snot onto my bloodied palms. The pain and effort made my vision blur, but I could breathe again.

In the dim light, I examined my body. My left knee was swollen and covered with a prune-colored bruise. More blotches dotted my legs, along with numerous scratches and cuts, none of which looked particularly deep. There was a gash on my left forearm that was more worrisome, running from the crook of my elbow all the way down to my wrist. It needed stitches. Then there were the puncture wounds the pterodactyl had made in my shoulders and back. They ripped and tore every time I moved. I patted the back of my head and found a cut there, as well. It didn't feel deep, but it was wide, and still bleeding. Knots and bumps had sprouted all over my scalp, and I wondered if I had a concussion. It was certainly probable.

"Not good," I muttered. My tongue snagged on a broken tooth. "Not good at all."

My voice echoed in the darkness.

*All ... all ... all ...*

Tending to my wounds was obviously my first priority, but all of my gear was back with the rescue party. I gingerly patted my pockets, looking for any aid I might have on me that I'd forgotten about, but they were empty. Worse, so was my holster. It had come undone at some point during my fall, and my pistol was now gone again.

Injured and defenseless, I slowly tottered to my feet. My groans echoed off the walls. Every time I turned my head, spasms ran down my neck and spine, so I moved my entire body in the direction I wanted to look, studying my surroundings. It turned out I wasn't in a cavern after all. At least, not a traditional one. Neither was I in any sort of artificial construct. During my time in the Lost Level, I had seen evidence of an underground network of artificial tunnels. This was not one of those.

Instead, I found myself standing in the center of some sort of natural conduit, similar to a lava tube. Just like those cave-like channels left behind after flowing lava drains beneath the hardened surface of a lava flow, the tunnel had a rough, cylindrical shape. The curved walls were pockmarked with step marks and ledges, left behind after lava had drained, marking the depths it had flowed—the same way lava tubes back home were known to have. The floor was a crazy quilt of bizarre shapes. Portions of the rock were smooth. Others seemed to billow, as if the rock had been frozen while undulating. Still other sections resembled ropes or tentacles. There were no stalactites, stalagmites, or other protrusions. Indeed, other than the ledges along the walls and the strange texture of the floor, the tube was smooth and barren. I judged its width to be about thirty feet wide and maybe twenty feet tall at its highest point. Its possible construction left me perplexed. Obviously, this tube was part of the cliff I had tumbled down, which meant it was part of the mesa-like spire the pterodactyl nest had perched atop of. That outcropping of rock, massive as it had been, was certainly not a volcano. Nor had I seen anything resembling a volcano during my flight. How then, to account for this sanctuary? If it was indeed a lava tube, then where had the lava come from? And if it wasn't a lava tube, then what had created it?

In a sudden panic, I wondered if the pterodactyls could gain access to the tunnel, or if some other predator might lurk somewhere in the darkness. I stood still and listened, realizing that I could no longer hear the dinosaurs. Was it possible they had given up their search? It occurred to me that my escape, while lucky for me, might be bad news for the rest of my friends. What if the pterodactyls began hunting them next, to make up for the meal that had gotten away? I could only hope that, having seen Tomkin and me carried off into the sky, the rest of the rescue party would be on guard and ready for such an attack.

It hurt to walk, but I forced myself to do so anyway, further exploring my shelter. Moving meant that I hadn't yet given up, and given my condition, it was important to keep a psychological advantage. My body wanted to collapse. My mind urged me on for Kasheena and the others. I kept one hand against the wall to steady myself, and stumbled toward the light. The tube sloped gently upward before beginning a much steeper incline. I craned my head upward, wincing with pain, and saw that the tube itself hooked up and around, much like the end of a clothes hanger. I remembered the strange curved aspect of the cliff that I'd noticed just before my plunge. Apparently, I'd fallen into the hole and then tumbled and rolled around the curve before falling into the tube itself. Thinking about it made me dizzy, but at least now I understood why the sunlight was so filtered, and why the pterodactyls' cries had seemed so far away when I had first regained consciousness.

The only source of light was from the hole above. Sighing, I ascended the slope as far as I could, before it became a steep, almost vertical climb, and looked around for my pistol. I saw only splashes of blood on the rocks that I'd collided with during my fall. There was no way I could climb any further. Slumping my bleeding shoulders in defeat, I turned around and headed back down into the tube. Descending hurt worse than climbing up had and keeping my balance took all of my concentration.

When I'd reached the spot where I'd first woken up, I stood there, tottering back and forth on my aching legs, and debated what to do next. First aid had to be my primary concern, followed by rest. After that, I'd need to find water, and perhaps food. Resigned to the fact that my .45 was probably lost forever, I decided not to worry about weapons for now. If I needed to defend myself, I could make do with a rock or even my fists, although given my weakened state, it would probably be a short fight.

*Who am I kidding?* I thought. *I've failed, Kasheena. I'm sorry. I'm going to die here.*

Obviously, I didn't. If I had, I wouldn't be writing down this memoir on some accounting ledgers in the ruins of an office building—although, given some of the inexplicable things I've seen during my time in the Lost Level, I suppose it is possible that I could have died in that tunnel and still recounted these events.

But I came close. It was one of my grimmest moments in this dimension.

I decided to head further down the tube, away from the opening. That meant going further away from the light, but the area around me was barren and offered nothing useful. If there was anything to be found, it had to be deeper in the tunnel. My progress was slow. With each step, my knee swelled and stiffened more, and my wounds kept reopening, spilling fresh blood. I still felt cold, most likely, I now decided, from a mixture of blood loss and shock. In the aftermath of my capture, escape, and fall, the adrenalin remaining in my system was making me nauseous.

The tunnel was quiet, save for the echoes of my own pained breathing and my boots scuffling against the rocks. That silence seemed to deepen the further I went into the shadows. I stumbled along, one hand against the wall for guidance. Soon, the darkness became complete. I couldn't see anything ahead of me, and when I glanced back the way I'd come, the sunlight had vanished, as well. I moved slower now, wary of tripping over a rock or cranny and injuring myself even more. The tube seemed to slope steadily downward. It wasn't steep, but it was certainly noticeable, even in the dark.

There was no way of knowing how far I walked, but the pain in my knee grew excruciating and the darkness grew more oppressive. I tried focusing on Kasheena, but my thoughts became a confusing jumble of show tunes, commercial jingles, television themes, and movie quotes. Since first arriving in the Lost Level, I'd rarely thought about the pop culture I'd left behind, but I did so now, at the cusp of death. Things like that had always seemed so trivial and pointless, but now they felt important. I think they helped me to feel alive and to keep my fears at bay. I was surprised by just how much I remembered. I tried whistling a sitcom theme song, but my mouth was parched, so I sang it—actually it was more like croaking it—out loud, instead, accompanied by a chorus of echoes. That kept me going for a bit, but then I descended into mumbling and babbling, interspersed with sobs and pained gasps. Fatigue and shock reduced me to a quivering mess—a bleeding, moaning, shivering wraith haunting this subterranean chamber.

That's why, when I saw the flashing red light ahead of me, I thought it must be part of my delirium. I closed my eyes and shook my head. When I opened my eyes again, the light was still there, flickering off the walls of the tunnel. The pulsations had a steady rhythm, blinking every few seconds, lighting up the walls and floor with a disconcerting strobe effect—a dance club in Hell, except instead of music, there were only the echoes of my pained breathing. I slumped to my knees, dizzy, and then crawled forward.

As I got closer, I saw that the light was part of some type of metal box, which looked like a shipping container. The light was bright enough that I could make out this portion of the chamber with each flash. The box had been placed in a ruddy, cragged corner, up against the left side of the tunnel wall. It was approximately the same size as a standard military footlocker, but fashioned out of what appeared to be chrome steel. When I drew near enough to touch it, I determined that it wasn't steel at all, but some type of shiny, durable plastic. I'd never seen anything like it before. I ran my hands over it, trying to find a hasp or a lock, but the box was seamless. My bloody handprints seemed to evaporate off the surface. The red light itself was imbedded on top of the container, inside a circular depression, and covered with some sort of clear material that looked like glass, but wasn't.

When the light flashed again, I turned my head aside, not wanting to be blinded. That was when I noticed the corpse. It lay inside a narrow, twisting crevice on the tunnel floor. Feeling weak, I nevertheless crawled over to the crack, dropped down inside next to the cadaver, and investigated further each time the light flashed. The body was clad head to toe in an astronaut's uniform, similar to ones I remembered from my Earth. Above the right breast pocket was an embroidered patch that read EDF. Below that was a smaller patch that said USAF. A plastic identification card was clipped below the left breast. Above this on the uniform was stenciled *USSS LEMAY*. My curiosity grew, cutting through the pain. I knew that USAF stood for United States Air Force, and USS designated a ship, though I didn't know what the extra S might represent, and I had no idea what EDF designated.

I inched myself closer to the corpse. The walls of the crevice pressed against me, bringing a new bout of pain. The light blinked again, just as I was eye level with the astronaut's face shield, and I recoiled in disgust. Whoever this was, they hadn't been here very long. The suit itself was in great shape but the same couldn't be said of its owner. Instead of mummifying or being reduced to a skeleton, the person inside the suit had exploded, much like a piece of meat left to rot in a food container. My guess was that anaerobic bacteria had gone to work inside the sealed spacesuit, reducing the astronaut to something that resembled a thick, brown stew. Retching, I yanked the laminated card from the victim's breast, climbed out of the fissure, and crawled back over to the container. Then I sat there panting, waiting to either throw up, pass out, or simply die.

I paused a few minutes, and when none of those things happened and my nausea had subsided, I made a halfhearted attempt at investigating the box. There were no visible hinges or lock, and I couldn't find any way of opening it. I felt it all over, searching for a hidden hasp. Then I mumbled "Open sesame."

*Me ... me ... me ...* answered the echoes.

I waved my hand at the chest in frustration. The light blinked differently when I moved—stopping its rhythmic pulsating. Frowning, I put my hand down. The light began to flash again.

When I raised my hand a second time, the rhythm changed once more.

I glanced down at the identification badge. It showed a color photograph of a man with a serious expression and a military haircut, wearing a helmetless spacesuit just like the one the skeleton was melting in. Next to that was the name *Colonel Elliott McKinnon* and the designations *United States Space Ship Lemay* and *Earth Defense Force*. Beneath that was an expiration date for the card itself, which read 12/21/16. Obviously, McKinnon had to be from an alternate universe, where by the year 2016, America had its own fleet of spaceships. Either that, or he was from my Earth, and the government and NASA hadn't been forthcoming about our advancements in space exploration.

Head spinning, I waved at the light, and again, it blinked. Then I held up the card and made sure the beam of light hit it. The light went out, then it came back on and stayed on. Its color had gone from red to a soft white. It wasn't bright, but it dispelled the darkness well enough for me to see easier. I heard a slight thrumming sound and then the container opened, the top slowly lifting up and backward with a hiss of compressed air. Then the movement stopped. I dragged myself over to the box and peered inside. My eyes widened, and now that the flashing had ceased, my head cleared.

"Holy shit ..."

*It ... it ... it ...*

One by one, I began to remove and inspect the contents, spreading them out around me on the cavern floor. There was a thin blanket sealed inside a clear cellophane wrapper, a second blanket fashioned from some sort of reflective, silver material, sealed packets and tubes of what I assumed to be food supplements, a pistol like nothing I'd ever seen before, a combat knife with a ten-inch serrated steel blade, and most importantly, a white plastic box that rattled when I shook it. The box had a big red cross painted on the lid. Unless Colonel McKinnon's dimension was drastically different from mine, that symbol meant a first aid kit.

My hands shook as I fumbled with the hasp, leaving smears of blood all over the plastic. The cavern began to spin. I ducked my chin onto my chest and took several deep breaths. When my vision cleared and I felt more stable, I rummaged through the kit. There were bandages and tubes of oral antibiotics and creams and an assortment of other things, but I brushed these aside and snatched up a bottle of antiseptic. Gritting my teeth, I poured it over my wounds. The pain was incredible, and I shook, sputtering aloud. My sense of determination returned, along with my resolve. Upending the bottle, I doused myself again, hissing through my clenched teeth. When I was finished, and the stinging had subsided, I ripped open the cellophane and used the blanket to pat my wounds dry. Then I searched through the kit again, looking for sutures or staples, or even an old-fashioned needle and thread. I didn't find any of those things, but I did find several tubes labeled as MEDICAL STRENGTH ADHESIVE in small black letters, followed by what I assumed was a serial or product number. This was better than sutures or thread. Back on my Earth, super glue and other high strength industrial adhesives had been invented for use on the battlefield. It was only later that we'd figured out they were also great at gluing broken toys and pottery back together. I pulled the cap off the tube, but there was no visible opening, so I used the combat knife to cut it open. A clear liquid seeped out. My eyes watered as a strong chemical smell drifted up from the container. I sat the knife aside and picked up the tube, being careful not to get the glue on my fingers. Then I applied it to one of the smaller lacerations on my arm. The pain was intense, but also freeing. Things seemed to come back into focus. The chemical stench grew stronger. I squeezed my skin together, amazed at how quickly the adhesive bonded. Within two minutes, the wound was sealed. I repeated the process over and over again. I had some difficulty with the injuries on my back, but did the best I could. The glue burned, and I had to pause several times and wait for the pain to subside, but eventually, the tube was empty and my cuts were closed. At least I wouldn't have to worry about bleeding to death. Finished, I applied some cream and bandaged my wounds as best I could. Finally, I tore open one of the tubes of antibiotics and swallowed several doses.

"Okay," I gasped. "I'm not going to die."

*Die ... die ... die ...*

"Shut up, echoes."

Leaning my back against the supply chest, I closed my eyes and waited to see who was right—me or the echoes.

I fell asleep, still waiting.

I dreamed of Kasheena, but instead of being here in the Lost Level together, we were living back on my world and my reality. She had a job as a realtor and wore skirts and heels instead of animal skins. I was going bald and had developed a pot belly. Our dear departed friend, Bloop, lived in a doghouse in our backyard, and had a long-running grudge against our faceless dream neighbor's poodle. At one point in the dream, Bloop used his prehensile tail to seize the dog and jerk it up over the fence. Then he pounced on the poodle, ripping into it with his teeth. He looked up at me, grinning, his teeth and blue fur stained with blood.

I awoke confused and ravenous. Panicked, I scrambled around in the low light, forgetting where I was. Then my throbbing knee brought it all back to me. I swallowed another dose of antibiotics and doctored my wounds again. The glue seemed to be holding. None of them had reopened while I slept. Then I examined the white plastic food packets. Like the surgical adhesive, each of the tubes had their contents stenciled on the side in small, black letters, followed by a serial number. I chose four labeled PEAS, ROAST BEEF, ORANGES, and—more dubiously—WATER. Using my teeth to tear open the latter, I experimented with the contents. Instead of liquid, the container was filled with a clear gel. I squeezed a drop of it onto the tip of my tongue. It was odorless and tasteless, but my mouth immediately filled with saliva, as if I'd just had a sip of water. My stomach rumbled. I squeezed the rest of the gel into my mouth, and then tried the peas—which turned out to be a green paste. The oranges and roast beef followed. None of them tasted like their advertised counterparts, but they weren't terrible, either. If anything, they were just bland. Despite the meager portions, I was amazed to find that I felt full after I'd squeezed out the last drop of roast beef. The rumbling in my stomach subsided. Satisfied, I rested some more, until the throbbing in my knee faded.

I occupied myself by cautiously studying the pistol. It was manufactured out of metal, but the steel felt somewhat different than that of any weapon I'd ever held before. Obviously, it had belonged to the astronaut, but the only space weapon I was familiar with was the Russian-made TP-82—a triple-barreled, deluxe, all-in-one handgun with a built-in machete and shovel that cosmonauts had carried into space for decades. They'd been meant for use in survival situations, should a cosmonaut land somewhere in the wilderness. This weapon looked nothing like those. The lone barrel was thicker than that of any handgun I'd ever seen, and there were no hidden compartments or extra weapons in the butt. Unlike the TP-82, the stock wasn't an astronaut's version of a Swiss Army knife. Perhaps most telling was the fact that the pistol didn't have anywhere to load ammunition. There was no cylinder, like on a revolver, and no magazine, like on a semi-automatic pistol, let alone anything resembling a magazine release. Indeed, the weapon had no other buttons, levers or switches at all, save the trigger. There was no safety, and no sights.

I turned it over in my hands and squinted at the tiny print. Stamped on the side was a designation that read *Taurus Corona SWDEW*, followed by a serial number. I was familiar with Taurus, of course. They were a gun manufacturer. I assumed Corona was a name for the model. I pondered over SWDEW for a moment, and then wondered if the last three letters stood for Direct Energy Weapon. Traditional firearms can operate in space, of course. Fires can't burn in an oxygen-less vacuum, but the gunpowder in bullets didn't need a fire to ignite them. Ammunition of the modern era contained a chemical oxidizer that triggered the firing of the round. The problem with shooting a standard bullet in space, however, was Newton's third law—for every action, there is an equal and opposite reaction. Fire a gun in outer space, and the force exerted on the bullet imparts an equal, opposing force on you. The bullet moves forward and you move backward. Then you and the bullet are both floating through space. That didn't happen with a direct energy weapon—at least not in any of the science articles or science-fiction stories I'd read. A weaponized laser, in theory, would produce a tight, synchronized wavelength of light pulses that would make holes in whatever they hit.

If this was a laser pistol, I was in no condition to test fire it or figure out how the weapon operated. I set it aside, and turned my attention back to the dead astronaut. It occurred to me that Colonel McKinnon's spacesuit might have more gear or items hidden in his pockets. The idea of disturbing his corpse made my stomach turn, but I needed to be thorough. I crawled over to his body and examined him closer. The front of his suit had three Velcro-sealed pockets, but all of them were empty. I wondered if there might be some back pockets. McKinnon's remains sloshed around inside his uniform as I rolled him over. The spacesuit had no back pockets, but I found something else. The astronaut had three items beneath him—a small notebook, a pen, and the smashed remains of some kind of electronic device. I examined the latter first. After assembling some of the fragments, I figured out that it was either a communicator or a recorder. It was similar to a cellular phone, but much smaller and thinner.

My wounds started to ache again. Retrieving the notebook, I crawled back over to the chest, spread out the blanket across the tunnel floor, and then laid down. I opened the notebook to the first page, and then, in the soft light, began to read.

# [ 9 ]
## THE FINAL TESTAMENT OF COLONEL ELLIOTT MCKINNON

I dropped the comp and now it's smashed all to hell, so I'll have to finish this by hand. That's not easy, because my hands are shaking. I think I might be in shock.

Wachowski, if you're reading this, you used to give me shit for carrying around old school books and notebooks and pens, but I'm glad now that I did. Without the comp, this will have to suffice.

Still no search party, and I still don't know where I am. Last readings from the comp were ... well, there weren't any readings. No latitude. No longitude. No magnetic north. Nothing since the test craft shot through the wormhole. According to the comp, I not only dropped off the grid—I'd dropped out of existence. But I already told you about all of that in the video I sent.

My busted leg is swollen up to about twice its size now. I should have taken off the rest of my suit when I took off my helmet. Now, there's no way I can remove it, except maybe by cutting through the fabric, and we all know how tough this material is.

Anyway, if you guys are reading this, then that means you

found me. You've already watched the first half, unless it got lost when I sent it. And who knows? Maybe it did. I'm lost. Maybe my digital transmissions are lost, too? But I'm going to assume you got my video, because there's not enough room in this notebook to write it all down again, and even if there was, I don't feel like repeating myself. And, to be honest, it makes me feel better to believe somebody received it. It makes me feel less alone.

So, yeah. After protecting and ensuring the continued existence of the Mars colony for four years (that's the maximum duty for non-terrestrial officers and enlisted forces on Mars, because after that, the constant radiation becomes an issue, even underground), I transferred back out to the fleet, back aboard the *USSS Lemay*. That was my first duty station off-Earth, and it felt good to come back to it again. I was surprised by all the new faces, though. A lot more newbies, fresh to the program and enjoying their enlistments, had been assigned while I was on Mars.

Soon after, I was asked to pilot the test craft through that wormhole out past Io. And you know the rest of the story. I made it through the wormhole and crashed here—wherever here is.

I can't remember if I said this in the video or not, but I am pretty sure I saw a dinosaur out there, flying in the sky. It was only a glimpse, and then I crashed. Maybe it was a hallucination. But I can't be sure.

Nobody is going to find me, are they? Even if they track the beacon onboard the craft, it's going to take them to the crash site. When they don't find me there, how will they know where to look? I'm underground. The second tracking beacon sewn into my suit isn't going to work through all this rock. It won't even show up on their scanners. I should have never left the site. If I hadn't, then my damn leg wouldn't be broken. It was a stupid idea, looking for a place to shelter. I should have left my gear at the crash and sheltered in place there.

Regrets? Sure, I have them. I wish I hadn't been so gung

fucking ho about my country and our mission priorities. I wish that I'd started a family, or at least had someone in my life. But I don't know how that's possible. It definitely wasn't doable after I joined. That's why they pick us. We fit the profile. No parents, no spouses, no kids. We can't have anyone to blab the truth to. Nobody we can tell that the American space program run by NASA is a sham, and has been since Eisenhower brought it into existence back in 1958. Nobody to tell that those projects like Gemini, the *Apollo* moon missions, and the Space Shuttle were all just publicity stunts. Oh, I'm not saying they were faked. On the contrary, they were real. The *Apollo* guys didn't film that in a Hollywood studio with Stanley Kubrick behind the camera like those nuts online believe. That's not the conspiracy. They really did land on the moon. But they weren't the first Americans there. That shit was done for the public. We'd already established two American bases on the moon by the time the public saw Neil Armstrong take his first steps on the surface. The United States space program existed long before people suspect.

How can you have a family when you're a part of something like this? How can you have someone to love when you'd have to lie to them every day? How would that relationship even work, when you spend most of your time off planet as part of the clandestine parallel space program run by the United States Department of Defense? Nobody knows it exists. Not Congress, and certainly not the American public. Nobody knows Russia and China have their own versions, either.

I would sound like a crazy person if I talked about the history of this conspiracy. Operation Paperclip, the Nazi Bell, the F-117A *Nighthawk*, the *Dyna-Soar*, the manned orbital laboratories, Project Horizon, the secret Space Shuttle bases in Colorado and New Mexico, the Mars landings and subsequent colonies, the outpost on Europa, the fleets, what happened to the *USSS*

*Hillenkoetter*, the Io probe ... How would I ever tell anyone about any of that?

Well, I couldn't. If I did, I'd be condemning myself—and anyone else I told—to death.

And now, as a result, I'm going to die alone. It will be like I never existed, because there's no one to miss me back home. I wish now that I had shared it with someone.

So, yes. I have regrets. And not having a family isn't the only one. I regret taking Trish to the prom back in the day. I should have taken her sister, instead. I think she and I could have had something together. Maybe if we had dated, instead of enlisting, I might have done something else instead. I regret having to give my dog to a shelter when I joined the Air Force.

But more than anything else, I regret the whole Indigo Skyfold operation and my involvement in it. Sure, that led to me being tapped for the Earth Defense Force, and I do believe we are doing good work in space, but Indigo Skyfold? Knowing what I know now? There was nothing good about spraying that toxic shit over the country. They'd have us fly specific routes, while satellites controlled the aerosol dispersal patterns. I know there were other pilots who rationalized it like that—saying we weren't really involved because the computers did all the work. All we did was make course corrections occasionally and handle the landings and takeoffs. The computers did the rest. But that's no justification. The DoD programmed those computers, and we knew damn well what was happening. Those eighteen months I flew for the program? I regret the hell out of those. National security my ass.

They told Kozeniewski that the stuff we were spraying would create a defensive atmospheric weapon shield, but that's bullshit. I know that now. I wish I was back home. Maybe I'd share it with the conspiracy people online, since it's not like I have anyone else to tell things to. Maybe I'd let them know that they are right, and that chemtrails are a real thing, heating the planet with elevated ultraviolet rays and toxic metals.

I'm tired now, and my leg hurts. I thought I heard voices a little while ago, but I think maybe it was just my breathing, echoing through this cave. I'm going to rest for a while, and finish this later. My head hurts, so I'm going to put my helmet back on. Then I won't hear anything if they return.

More later.

## [ 10 ]
## CITY OF DARKNESS, IN THE LIGHT

Except that there was no later. Colonel McKinnon's journal ended with the promise of more, but the rest of the pages were blank. I wondered again how long he'd been here. Despite his body's putrefaction, his spacesuit, gear, and journal were all still in remarkable shape. It was entirely possible that he had arrived not that long ago. If so, then there was a possibility that others from his timeline might come looking for him. I sat there for a long time, rereading what he'd written, and pondering the ramifications until fatigue wore me down. I spread the silver blanket out over the rocky floor and covered myself with the other blanket, which was still splattered with my blood from when I'd cleaned my wounds.

I fell asleep still mulling over the astronaut's story.

I must have been out for a long time, judging by the condition of my wounds and the hunger I felt upon waking again. I changed my bandages, noticing with some satisfaction that the cuts and punctures were well on their way to healing, with no signs of infection. I still ached, and my knee still troubled me, but I was no longer worried about dying. Indeed, I had more immediate concerns—rescuing Kasheena and the others and satisfying the gnawing urgency in my belly. I devoured what was left of the food, saving a few tubes of water for my impending journey, and then stood up, intent on testing out my legs. I walked back and forth in the tunnel, seeing if my knee would support my weight. It ached and throbbed, but I was able to move, albeit slower than my usual pace.

Satisfied that continuing my quest wouldn't leave me crippled, I then experimented with the pistol. After a few moments of study, I got it to fire. Amazingly, the weapon was soundless and had no recoil, emitting only a pulsating beam of laser light. I aimed it at the tunnel wall and watched as a small hole formed in the rock. As long as I squeezed the trigger, the pulses continued. When I let go, the firing stopped. I tried it again, aiming at the same spot. The rock around the hole began to heat up and the hole started to expand. I decided this would do nicely against the Anunnaki.

"Now I have a laser pistol," I said, mimicking Bruce Willis in *Die Hard*. "Ho, ho, ho."

*Ho ... ho ... ho ...*

"I've had enough of you, echoes. It's time to leave this place."

I shuffled back over to the container and debated how best to carry my newfound gear. I was still clad in the denim jeans I'd been wearing upon my arrival in the Lost Level. They'd been resewn several times during my stay in the village, and patched in spots with animal hide. They were threadbare and dirty, and my capture by the pterodactyl and subsequent fall had only worsened their condition. Briefly, I considered the astronaut's uniform, but the thought of donning that outfit with his slimy remains coating the interior was too much for me. Shrugging, I stuffed the water tubes into the front pockets of my jeans. I shoved the laser pistol in my waistband, and it fit securely. I wasn't worried about it misfiring. My experimentation with it had proven that the only way it could discharge was if someone squeezed the trigger, and that was protected with a guard. Remembering the combat knife, I glanced around the floor until I found it. I bent down to retrieve it, but the blade was stuck fast to the rocks. Confused, I tugged harder. It still wouldn't give. Then I remembered that I'd gotten some of the medical adhesive on it. I used another rock to pound it free, striking the hilt again and again. The blade was scarred from the effort, but otherwise okay. Since I had no sheath for it, I cut a strip off the blanket and tied one end around the hilt and the other around my belt loop. The first aid kit was too large to squeeze into my pockets, so I piled it, the reflective blanket, and Colonel McKinnon's journal into the center of the other blanket and drew the ends together, fashioning a crude sling-bag.

Finished, I stood looking down at Colonel McKinnon for a moment, somberly thanking him for his help. Then I began to walk. I knew it was futile to try to get out the way I'd come in, so my only choice was to head deeper into the tunnel. I closed the storage container before departing. The light went out, and then that monotonous red flashing began again. I limped along, favoring my injured knee and focusing on my footing. I'd survived against seemingly impossible odds, and it wouldn't do to trip and fall in a hole now, breaking my leg and ending up like the tunnel's other occupant.

The darkness deepened again as I moved farther away from the red light. Soon, I found myself surrounded by it, shuffling along blindly in the dark. I considered using the pistol to light my way, but I didn't know if that would drain its energy source or not. I opted instead to feel my way forward, and as a result, my progress slowed. I stumbled a few times, and my knee began to protest. Eventually, I had to stop and rest. I stood there panting, listening to my echoes. Having been away from darkness for so long, its presence now made me uncomfortable. It was easy for me to understand why our primitive ancestors feared it so much. It played tricks on my mind—turning the echoes of my breathing into the grunts of an unseen monster, lurking just beyond my reach. I had to force myself to continue forward, resisting the urge several times to turn around and return to the spot by the chest.

I don't know how long I hiked, but I was bathed in sweat and my knee began to swell. I was just about to take another break when I realized that there was light again. It still wasn't bright enough to see more than my hand right in front of my face, but there was definitely a source of illumination ahead. I pressed forward, and soon I saw a white circle of sunlight. I limped toward it for a long time, but seemed to draw no nearer. Frustrated, I quickened my pace. My knee throbbed, the pain increasing, but I gritted my teeth, determined to reach it.

Visibility increased as I got closer to the circle. It was an opening, and the light was coming from the sun! I threw aside caution now, ignoring my pain, and hurried toward it. The tunnel opened several hundred feet above the city I'd glimpsed before, but from a different vantage point. While in the clutches of the pterodactyl, I hadn't been sure the city belonged to the Anunnaki. Now, I saw them for myself. I stood there gasping, gripping the side of the cave mouth to keep myself from falling, and stared down into that bowl-like valley. Clinging tightly, I leaned out farther and spotted a ledge I could crawl out onto. I slithered along on my belly, wincing at the pain this caused, but cautious of being spotted. Then I watched as the snake men scurried about below. Seeing them filled me with anger and revulsion, but once again, I was impressed by the craftsmanship used in the construction of the buildings and spiraling towers. I wondered if they had built them, or if the city had existed before their arrival, and the Anunnaki had just taken them over. The only thing not built from stone or bricks were the half-dozen mud huts on the far side of the huge courtyard, set between one of the dome-shaped structures and that massive pit I'd spotted earlier. Each of the huts were guarded by two Anunnaki, who stood outside the entrances. I wondered if these huts were where the reptilians were holding Kasheena and the others. I spied for a long time, but unfortunately, saw no glimpse of our loved ones. Turning my attention to the pit, I couldn't guess at its purpose and was unable to determine anything else about it, other than that it seemed unfathomably deep and pitch black inside.

A few times while on the ledge, I heard the cries of a pterodactyl. Each time, I cowered against the rock, half-suspecting to be plucked from my perch and brought back to the nest again. But the sounds were more distant, and I never saw the beast. Still, I couldn't be that far from the nest. Since I couldn't exit the tunnel the way I'd come in, I would have to be careful during my descent—and mindful of threats from both above and below.

I spotted a small, rough footpath about ten feet below the ledge. I don't know what kind of creature made it, but it reminded me of the trails mountain goats make in those nature documentaries back on Earth—narrow, winding, and treacherous—but since the only other way down the mountainside was a sheer plummet, I decided to chance it. I dropped my gear down first and then lowered myself over the side, gritting my teeth against the pain. After a moment, I let go. The combat knife banged against my leg as I landed on my feet. The laser pistol fell out of my waistband, striking a rock, but didn't fire. Just as I'd suspected, the trigger guard protected against accidental discharges. I waited for a few minutes, letting the pain subside. Then I retrieved all my gear and started down the mountainside.

At first, my progress was excruciatingly slow. Still sore and stiff from my capture and subsequent fall, I took my time. But it has always been my experience that exercise and physical exertion have underappreciated value when it comes to healing, and this was no different. By the time I'd reached the halfway point in my descent, I felt noticeably better and quickened my pace. I still had to go carefully, however. There were times the path weaved between cracks and crevices that I couldn't fit through, so I ended up climbing around them instead. The worst moment was when the path wormed its way across a cliff face overlooking a deep, boulder-strewn chasm. The cliff itself was only about twenty feet across, after which the trail continued on solid ground, but I spent those harrowing twenty feet with my back against the cliff, inching along a ledge barely ten inches wide, with nothing else to protect me from a dizzying drop.

The city passed in and out of my sight as I descended. As I got closer to the ground, I was able to make out more details on the buildings, including a curious cuneiform lettering on many of their sides. The wedge-shaped letters were unlike anything I was familiar with. Some of the characters were similar to those on Akkadian, Elamite, and Old Persian clay tablets I'd seen translated during my occult studies, but I couldn't define anything from their usage, given that the rest of the symbols were utterly incomprehensible. It was the equivalent of spotting a few familiar vowels amidst a string of gibberish. I also began to see more details regarding the city itself. There were streets and avenues, and the courtyard was composed of paved stones, set carefully in place. I saw no gardens or cultivated vegetation, but a few sparse clusters of weeds grew here and there. The Anunnaki had a water source—a large cistern on the far edge of the city, built to catch rainwater. A small, shallow reservoir occupied a space beneath the cistern. It, too, looked manufactured, rather than naturally formed. There was no livestock. No pack animals or beasts of burden. I found myself wondering what the snake men ate. If they were similar to their reptilian cousins, were they carnivores, like an alligator or crocodile? Did they swallow their food whole, like a snake? The fact that I saw no crops led me to believe they probably weren't herbivores. Could they be insectivores, subsisting off whatever meager bugs this barren plain offered? No, it was more likely they were meat eaters—and given that they didn't have livestock around, my fear and dread over their plans for Kasheena and the others grew.

Halfway down the mountainside, I stopped briefly, allowing myself just enough time to fish a water tube out of my front pocket and down it in one squeeze. Then I continued on, following the trail. Twice more I heard the pterodactyl, but still saw no sign of the beast. The city loomed closer, and I began to worry about being spotted. There were lots of rocks and boulders and protrusions to hide behind, but if the Anunnaki had guards watching the path, or positioned in one of those tall spires, they'd have no problem spotting me amidst the stark landscape. I moved extra cautiously, sacrificing speed for stealth and trying to keep myself concealed, moving from one hiding place to the next, and crouching in between. Luckily, the path widened somewhat, and the ascent became less steep and rugged.

I had just passed by the sun-bleached skeleton of some dead animal and was rounding a bend, when I heard hushed voices from somewhere ahead of me. I knew it couldn't be the snake-men, since they didn't communicate audibly. Slowing down even more, I untied my combat knife and crept forward. As the voices got louder, I grinned, recognizing some of them. Sure enough, a second later, I heard a muffled bleating of what was undeniably a baby triceratops. Relaxing, I stood up and walked toward them. It turned out my friends were below me, at the bottom of a shallow ravine. The embankment sloping down to it was composed of shale rock, and a stone ledge on the other side provided some rare shade. The group was gathered beneath this, arguing about what to do next.

"This beast cannot follow us," Tolia insisted, pointing at

Fern. “She is clumsy and noisy and we are close to the city. Also, she stinks.”

Ambrose sighed in obvious exasperation. “But we cannot send her back unaccompanied, madam.”

“I have told you, my name is not Madam. My name is Tolia.”

“I beg your pardon, then, of course. However, I cannot in good conscience turn Fern away. Nor am I certain she would leave us anyway.”

“She’ll leave in a hurry if I stick her in the rear with my sword,” Trut grumbled.

“And I shall stick you a second later,” Ambrose replied. “Do not test me, sir.”

“We are wasting time,” Karune said. “While we stand here and argue over this ... this ... thing, our loved ones suffer in the clutches of the snake men! My child and my sister—”

Karenk held up his hands. “Aaron said the baby only squeals when Ambrose gets too far away. If she stays with us—”

“Aaron isn’t here,” Tolia said, “and I will not choose this thing’s life over the lives of our people.”

The exchange was growing heated. I was certain I could cool both sides down, but first I needed to make my presence known without startling them. They were all on edge, and if I blundered into the ravine and surprised them, there was a good chance my own tribe would kill me before they realized who I was. Stowing my knife again, I stood up and walked to the edge of the ravine. My shadow stretched over them, but no one noticed. I cleared my throat. Karenk gasped, and they all turned toward me, weapons in hand. I raised my arm in greeting, and started to take a step forward, but my injured leg wobbled and suddenly, I was tumbling down the embankment, leaving a cloud of dust in my wake. Tiny pieces of shale cut and scratched me, and I landed in their midst, rolling to a stop on my back. I lay there panting, trying not to cry out in pain.

All of the tribe members stared at me in disbelief. Flik opened his mouth to speak, and then shut it again, blinking instead.

"Can somebody give me a hand?" I groaned.

Karenk reached out with one massive paw and helped me to my feet. As I steadied myself, he clapped me on the back, right where the pterodactyl's talons had gripped me. I nearly fell over again. Wincing in pain, I bit my lip to keep from crying out. Still, no one spoke. They simply gaped at me, as if I were an apparition. Then, Ambrose began to laugh.

"The hardest tumble a man can take is to fall over his own bluff," he chuckled, "but that might be the second hardest tumble I have ever witnessed."

"Hello, Mr. Bierce."

"Hello yourself, Aaron."

"We did not expect to see you again," Tolia said. "How are you alive?"

I shrugged. "It's a long story. Let me sit down and I'll tell you all about it."

"And Tomkin?" Marta asked. "Is he alive, as well?"

I shook my head, and they grew silent again. They watched me sit, stiffly, and Tolia stepped forward.

"You are injured?"

"I'll be okay. I just need to rest. Everybody sit down."

When they did, I distributed the rest of the water tubes and doctored my fresh wounds with the first aid kit. Tolia and Ambrose helped me with the hard-to-reach injuries on my back. Then I told them about what had happened—the pterodactyl nest and Tomkin's fate, my escape into the tunnel, and an abbreviated version of what I discovered there. I also told them about what I had observed of the city. It turned out I'd had a much better view of it from my vantage point. They had only seen it in glimpses as they approached.

"So, what's the plan?" I asked Tolia.

"I do not know," she replied. "We were debating that when you ... arrived. Karune scouted ahead. This ravine leads directly to the city's edge. There is a place to hide and observe them, but she says that sneaking in from that direction would be impossible."

I turned to Karune. "Did you see anything else? Any sign of our people?"

"No, Aaron." She lowered her head and mumbled. "I did not spy long. I became afraid the snake men would see me."

"That's okay," I assured her. "I think we're all afraid, and with good reason."

"Indeed," Ambrose agreed, scratching Fern on the bony plate between her eyes. "Fear has no brains, young Karune. The dismal witness that it bears and the cowardly counsel that it whispers to us are always unrelated."

Karune frowned. "I do not understand your words."

"Neither do I," Flik agreed.

Ambrose's bushy eyebrows furrowed. "Even here, I must suffer the barbs of critics."

I tottered to my feet and nodded at Karune. "Can you show me this spot?"

"Aaron," Karenk said gently, "you should let me go instead. You need to rest."

"No," I insisted. "I need Kasheena and the rest of our people. I'm fine. Karune and I will scout ahead, and have a look. Then we'll come back here and make plans."

I stowed my gear with the group, taking along only my weapons. Then I followed Karune through the ravine. I struggled at times to keep up with her. As we neared the city, she slowed down, creeping forward. I glimpsed the spires ahead of us, jutting up from the valley. We emerged onto a broad, flat ledge overlooking the city from a height of about twenty feet. There was a gentle slope beneath it, and it would have been easy enough for us to ascend into the city proper, but the slope terminated at an empty expanse, and we would have had to cross one hundred yards of open terrain, with no cover or concealment. Short of marching in with an army, there was no way we could sneak into the city from this point. We hunkered down behind a jumble of boulders and I gazed around the rest of the valley. I spotted a dirt road to the west, between two large hills. Presumably the road led out onto the plain. The rest of the city was bordered on all sides by cliffs and hillsides, rendering it inaccessible except by air.

"Not good," I whispered. "The only way in is via that road or this slope beneath us."

Karune nodded. "Both seem foolish, given our meager numbers."

"Yes," I agreed. "If we choose either, we're only going to get captured or killed."

"If we got captured, then perhaps they would put us with the other prisoners."

"Probably, but there's not much good we'd do them if we were captured, too, Karune."

"At least we would all be together."

"I know you're worried about your sister and your child, but I want a better reunion for you than captivity, Karune."

I watched as the Anunnaki went about their various tasks. I didn't get the sense that there was any sort of caste system or different classes among them. They were more akin to a hive of bees—drone workers going about their labors, and doing so with a single-minded purpose. Some of them carried weapons. Others carried tools, or went about empty-handed. All of them were dressed. Many wore the tanned hides of humans and animals. Others wore clothing fashioned from fibers and cloth. What disturbed me most was the silence. They made no sound as they moved throughout the city. Occasionally, various individuals or groups would stop and stare at each other, communicating telepathically, but there were no verbal cues or spoken words. One thing I noticed is how all of them avoided the giant pit in the middle of the courtyard. I got the sense that they did so out of some sort of reverence, rather than fear or apprehension.

I changed position, moving to another part of the ledge so that I could better view the mud huts. Karune turned her attention to these, as well. We watched for a long time, and saw no movement other than a changing of the guard. Then, just as I was about to tell Karune we should head back and rejoin the others, another snake-man arrived, carrying a wicker basket. He nodded at the guards and went into one of the huts. After a moment, I heard a voice, carrying to me on the wind, easily audible in that oppressive silence. Karune gripped my shoulder, indicating she heard it—and recognized it—as well. Her fingertips brushed against my cuts, but I barely noticed, so intently was I focused on that voice.

It was the voice of Kasheena, and she was pissed off.

"You bring us water and food, but you won't untie us to eat it? Away with you!"

A pause.

"I said, go away. I will not be force fed by the likes of—"

Kasheena's protest faded, whether because the wind had shifted, or because her captors had somehow silenced her, I didn't know. My entire body thrummed with rage. I forgot about my injuries and my pain. Gone was my exhaustion. I didn't think about the rest of the rescue party, waiting for us further back up the ravine. I barely acknowledged Karune, even as her grip grew tighter. My vision narrowed, and my heart pounded. I began to hyperventilate. My arms and legs tingled as if asleep. Brandishing the laser pistol, I stood up, preparing to charge in. Karune grappled with me, trying to pull me back down. I swatted her away, growling.

"Kasheena is down there!"

Karune scurried backward, eyes wide with panic. Then, as I turned away from her and back toward the city, she punched me in the testicles. The effect was instantaneous. My breath whooshed out of me and my knees buckled. I fell to the ground, cracking my elbow on the stone. My hand went numb and the laser pistol skidded from my grasp. I tried to yell at her, but could only manage a wheeze. Ropes of saliva dripped from my lips. Curling my legs up to my chest, I lay there squirming, cradling my testicles. The pain set in, starting in my groin, spreading to my stomach, and then radiating throughout my entire body.

"I am sorry, Aaron."

I could barely hear Karune over the pounding in my head.

"I know you want to save Kasheena," she continued, "but this is not the way. You have said so yourself. We all have people among those prisoners. My sister and my child—my only child—are down there. I will not see them jeopardized because you rushed in."

I croaked a response and tried not to throw up.

"I respect you, Aaron. I remember when Kasheena first brought you to us. You were strange—as strange as this new man, Bierce, who now travels with us. You were an outsider, but in time, you became one of us. Your respect earned everyone's respect. You are a leader now. I would follow you anywhere, and I am not the only one. But I will not follow you on a fool's errand —not when the lives of my loved ones hang in the balance. Now, collect yourself, and let us craft a better plan."

I took a deep breath and nodded. Karune knelt down next to me, staring at me intently.

"You will not hit me?"

I shook my head and whispered, "No. You're right."

She held out her hand. I clasped it and let her pull me to my feet. Then I crouched for a bit, hands on my knees, and waited for the pain to subside. When I'd caught my breath, I stood up, and nodded at her again.

"Thanks, Karune. You are absolutely right. I'm sorry. My anger got the best of me."

"And you are not angry with me?"

"No. You did what you had to do. And besides, it's not the worst thing that's happened to me on this trip. The pterodactyl was tougher."

Grinning, she clapped my shoulder and squeezed. The pain was so intense that my vision blurred. Rather than reminding her that I'd recently been injured, I simply returned the gesture and apologized again. Then we snuck out of the area and made the return trip back through the ravine to rejoin our friends. Karenk was guarding one end of the camp and Marta guarded the other. Everyone else was resting. They stirred when we arrived, looking at us eagerly.

"Well?" Tolia stood, hands on hips.

I shrugged. "Our people are there. The Anunnaki have them imprisoned in a series of mud huts on the outskirts of the city."

"You know this for sure?" Trut asked.

"Yes. We heard Kasheena."

"We did," Karune confirmed. "And judging by what she said, at least some of the others are alive, as well."

A chorus of relieved sighs and gasps greeted this.

"What do we do?" Shlak asked. "How do we free them?"

Kneeling, I drew my combat knife and motioned at them all to gather around me. When they had, I began using the tip of my blade to sketch out the city's outline in the dirt. "There are two ways in—this ravine and a dirt road. If we use either of them, we'd have to cross an awful lot of open space before we reached the huts. There's no cover, nothing to hide behind. If just one of the enemy spots us, we'll be cut down or caught before we ever reach the prisoners."

Trut squinted with his one eye. "What about from above?"

"Not unless we had wings," Karune answered.

"So, it is hopeless," Flik sighed. "All this way for nothing."

"Not for nothing," Marta said. "Our loved ones are near. We will find a way."

"I will cause a distraction," Karenk said. "The rest of you will wait at the mouth of the ravine. I will approach the city from the road. While I battle the snake men, the rest of you can sneak in and free our people."

"That is ridiculous," Ambrose argued.

Karenk smirked. "You have never seen me fight, old one. I can slay dozens before they kill me. Their numbers shall crash upon me like water on a stone."

"If I can gain high ground," Tolia said, "I can assist Karenk with my bow."

They all began to talk at once, arguing with each other. Disturbed by the commotion, Fern whinnied nervously, and pushed tight against Ambrose. I waved for silence, and when I had everyone's attention, the baby dinosaur relaxed.

"I can't let you do that, Karenk, but you are on the right track."

He frowned. "Track?"

"Yes. What we need is a diversion. A distraction."

"What we need," Shlak muttered, "is an army."

Tolia cocked her head. "What do you suggest, Aaron?"

"Well, that depends. Did any of you happen to bring rope along when we left the village?"

"Aye," Trut said. "I have coils of rope in my pack."

"How much?"

He shrugged. "Enough to reach the top of yonder cliff, if we had to."

"Good," I replied. "Then I know where we can get a distraction ... and an army. Like Karune said, we need wings."

And then I told them what I had in mind. They were incredulous at first, but in the end, I was able to convince them. As far as plans go, it wasn't a good one. Indeed, looking back on it now, the whole thing seems so stupid. Maybe I wasn't thinking clearly. After all, I was exhausted and still recovering from my injuries—but it was the only other option I could come up with that didn't involve Karenk or another member of our party sacrificing themselves on the slight possibility that it might distract the Anunnaki long enough for us to free the prisoners. At least I was smart enough not to attempt it by myself. I was well aware of just how much punishment my body had undertaken on this journey, and how close to my limits I had come. Ultimately, I chose Flik for his youthful agility, and Karenk for his brute strength. For what I had planned, I would need them both.

As everyone began to prepare for their roles, Ambrose pulled me aside. I gave him Colonel McKinnon's journal for safekeeping. I had already given the first aid kit and my blanket-sling to Tolia. Ambrose accepted the journal and promised to take good care of it. Then he fell silent. His expression was troubled.

"You don't have to go through with this, you know?" I stared into his eyes. "You don't owe us anything. You and Fern can still get out of it. No hard feelings."

"The only hard feelings I am experiencing are anger and regret with myself."

"How so?"

"I should be making that climb with you."

I paused, wanting to choose my words carefully so I wouldn't offend him. "Ambrose, while I appreciate the gesture, I don't think—"

"Spare me the platitudes, Aaron." He held up his hand. "You're squirming like a worm on a fishhook. I know I am too old to accompany you. That is what I am angry about. Although, truth be told, I am not sure how much assistance I will be here on the ground, either."

"You're a soldier," I reminded him. "An officer. If you choose to stay and fight, then my people are going to need your guidance."

He glanced back at the tribe. "They're all better warriors than I ever was. Especially that woman, Tolia. Were I thirty years younger ..."

"So, does that mean you're staying?"

"I never thought to do otherwise. I always said that friendship was a ship big enough for two in fair weather, but only one in foul. You and your people have taught me otherwise. For that, I am grateful."

Grinning, I shook his hand. "Thank you, Mr. Bierce."

"Thank you, Aaron. It has been a pleasure making your short acquaintance. I hope that we have more time."

"Yeah." I let go of his hand and shrugged.

His bushy eyebrows furrowed. "You do not believe that we will, do you?"

"No," I admitted. "I suspect this is going to go terribly awry ... but I don't know what else to do."

"I have always endeavored to see things as they are, rather than as they ought to be. In this case, I think we all see how things are. Your options are extremely limited, and yet you are attempting, rather than giving in to despair. Sometimes, that is all you can do, Aaron."

I nodded.

"Well ..." He dusted off his sleeves and shook my hand again. "Goodbye, Aaron Pace. It is my sincere hope that we meet again when this is all over with. If not, then as I said, it has been my distinct pleasure. I wish you luck. I will do what I can down here. If these snake men stand me up against that canyon wall and cut me to ribbons, please know that I think that is a pretty good way to depart this life. It certainly beats dying of old age, or disease, or falling down the cellar stairs back home. If I had my way, I would rather fall down yonder cliff. You be careful during your ascent."

"It's not the climb I'm worried about," I replied. "It's when we come back down. I just hope it works."

"And I as well."

"Take care, Ambrose."

I wrapped Trut's rope up in the reflective blanket and made sure my laser pistol and knife were secure. When we had all finished our preparations, Karune led Tolia, Shlak, Trut, Marta, and Ambrose along the ravine, going in the direction they had originally come. Fern trotted along behind them, grunting softly. We had given Ambrose all of the rest of our rations, hoping steady and measured feeding would keep the baby triceratops quiet long enough for my plan to work—or fail. Karune was to lead them to the road we had spotted earlier and find a place to conceal themselves until we returned with the distraction. We watched them go. Then Karenk, Flik, and I began to climb back up the mountain, heading for the tunnel.

# [ 11 ]
## THE KIDNAPPING

I don't know why, but the ascent seemed easier to me than my descent had been. We made much better time, as well. Maybe it was because I didn't want to appear weak or unsteady in front of Flik and Karenk. Perhaps it was because I was concerned that Fern would give the location of the others away, and that they would be captured or killed before we could do our part. Or maybe it was just the fact that I had heard Kasheena's voice and knew for certain that she was alive. Whatever the case, I spurred myself on—winded and tired and in constant pain, but determined nevertheless. Finding the way was easy. I just followed the same trail I'd used before, and tried not to fall off the cliffs or slide down the mountainside.

When we reached the rocky ledge overlooking the city and gained access to the tunnel opening, I called for a brief rest. Both Karenk and Flik milled about nervously, glancing into the darkness. They whispered to each other, recoiling from the tunnel as if it were a serpent poised to strike. It occurred to me that neither of them were used to such a thing. Both men had been born here in the Lost Level and had lived here all their lives, and as a result, they had never known the true, all-encompassing absence of sunlight.

"Stick close to me," I advised. "You will be unable to see, and the floor is uneven, so be careful where you step."

Flik stared into the darkness. His entire body was tense. His breath came in short, shallow gasps.

"Flik," I said gently. "You going to be okay?"

"Can it ..." He licked his lips nervously. "Can it hurt us?"

"The darkness? No. It can't hurt us."

"But, what is it?"

"It's just the opposite of light, Flik. It can't hurt you, but it can leave you disoriented. Like I said, when we get in there, just go slow and watch where you step. The tunnel does weird things with sounds. You might hear your own breathing echoing back to you, and think it's something else, but I've been through here already, and there's nothing else alive in there. It's safe. Okay?"

Taking a deep breath, Flik nodded. I turned to Karenk, noticing then that this mountain of a man was trembling.

"Karenk? Understood?"

He turned to me, and I saw that all the color had drained from his face.

"I understand, Aaron," he whispered, "but I am more frightened right now than at any time in my life."

"I know you are." I smiled, trying to reassure him. "It's okay, Karenk. I promise, there is nothing inside this tunnel that can hurt you. Just stay with me, and I'll get us through to the other side."

"As you wish, Aaron. Have I ... have I ever told you just how much I admire you?"

I shrugged. "It's okay, buddy."

"No, it is not. When you first came to us, I wished to be with Kasheena. I saw you as a competitor. Do you remember?"

"I do. But that's all in the past, Karenk."

"Aye. Perhaps it is. But my respect for you is here, in the present. Do you understand?"

Swallowing, I nodded. "I feel the same way, my friend."

I stood slowly and shook his hand, then walked inside the tunnel. Karenk and Flik shuffled along behind me. The shadows deepened. The air grew cooler. Soon, the darkness engulfed us. Both of them gasped, faltering.

"Stow your weapons," I said, "and hold hands."

Whimpering, they did as I'd said, and we proceeded forward in a human chain. Flik was in the middle, for which I was glad. He squeezed my hand tight enough to be painful. I could only imagine how excruciating Karenk's grip would have been. I led them deeper into the tunnel, listening to their panicked breathing, and tried to project confidence and assurance. They shuffled unsteadily, tripping a few times. I won't recount our entire journey through the underground chamber, because it would be repetitive and because I'm running out of space in this accounting ledger. Suffice to say, much like the trip back up the mountainside, we seemed to make much better time than I had on my initial trip—even with Flik and Karenk's hesitation. I only hoped that our return through this passage would be even quicker.

Karenk began to hyperventilate.

"Stay with us," I urged. "It's okay."

"The floor," he whispered. "The texture is so strange. It feels as if we are walking on snakes."

"We're not," I promised. "Just focus on putting one foot in front of the other."

Karenk took several deep, shuddering breaths. I led them forward, step by step. Slowly, he ceased hyperventilating.

Eventually, we saw the flashing red light from Colonel McKinnon's storage locker. Upon spotting it, both of my companions stopped so suddenly that I stumbled. I tried to push forward, but they yanked me backward.

"What is that?" Flik gasped.

"It's okay," I answered. "It's just a light."

"But it is red! You see? It is unnatural. Light is not red."

"This one is. Just try not to stare directly into it. The flashes will make your head hurt."

"I do not know if I can look away," Karenk mumbled.

I urged them onward. When we reached the astronaut's corpse I called for another halt, thinking that a few moments spent in the dim glow might help them both further acclimate. It did. Both men sat there, huddled together. Unfortunately, we couldn't linger long. I reminded them that people were counting on us, and time was of the essence. Reluctantly, they joined hands again and we continued on our way.

After a while, sunlight began to filter down into the tunnel, and I knew that we must be nearing the other side. Flik and Karenk began to slowly relax as things got brighter. Karenk even began to experiment with the echoes of his voice. Soon, he and Flik both laughed nervously. I let them go, glad they were distracted. It wasn't until we neared the end that I cautioned them to whisper again.

When we reached the curved opening, I nodded at Flik. "Think you can scale that?"

"I have climbed much more difficult slopes, Aaron. It will be easy."

"I hope you're right. Otherwise, this entire trek was pointless." I handed him the ropes. "Secure one of these when you reach the top. Remember, the nest is directly above the tunnel entrance, so be careful the birds don't spot you."

"Spot me?"

"See you."

"I understand."

He slung the rope coils around his neck and then bounded up the rocky slope, eagerly heading toward the sunlight. Karenk and I watched his ascent with some amazement. When he reached the top of the slope, Flik studied the curvature for a moment. Then, he leaped into the air and caught hold of the ledge with his fingertips. He dangled there for a moment, and then swung his legs up. My heart hammered in my throat, expecting him to slip and fall, but he didn't. Indeed, he seemed to cling to the roof like a spider, defying gravity, working his fingertips into unseen cracks and crevices, before scurrying upward and out of our sight. Dust and pebbles tumbled down out of the opening as he crawled further upward. For a while, we could still hear him. Then all went silent.

Karenk glanced at me, wide-eyed. "You were right to bring him along. Neither of us could have done that."

"I couldn't have," I admitted. "But you might have had a chance."

"No, I am strong, but with that strength comes clumsiness. My mother used to say I was as graceful as a thunder lizard in a fern grove."

"We had a similar saying where I came from—like a bull in a china shop."

"What is a china shop?"

Before I could explain, something rustled above us, echoing oddly through the chamber. Then a length of rope plummeted down. The other end was affixed beyond our field of vision.

"Son of a bitch," I whispered. "He did it."

Because of my injuries, I knew that I would climb slower than Karenk, so I opted to go first. By the time I reached the top, and felt the wind and sun on my face again, my muscles were shaking and I'd nearly lost all my strength. Stinging sweat ran into my eyes, blinding me. Noticing my distress, Flik grabbed my wrists and helped me out of the hole. I blinked the sweat away, and the world swam before me, tilting and listing like a boat at sea. It took a moment to get my footing and balance. While I did, Karenk made the climb and joined us.

I held a finger to my lips, cautioning them both, and then pointed upward, indicating the direction of the pterodactyl nest. We stood there, listening, and soon enough, heard what I was both dreading and hoping for—a deep, grating croak indicating that at least one of the parents were home.

"Okay," I whispered. "Remember, we can't just get eggs. We need live babies, too, so that the mother will hear their cries. If we can't get the parents to follow us, then this has all been for nothing."

Both of them nodded in understanding. Then I motioned at Flik to go ahead. He crept up the side of the cliff, once again seeming to find handholds and crannies where we could discern none. He tied the second rope off near the top, cowering against the cliff face as he did, so he wouldn't be seen. Flik tugged on the rope, making sure it was tight, and then motioned at us to climb up. This time, Karenk went first. I followed along after him, wincing in pain. When I was halfway up, we heard a rustling commotion above us. All of the babies began to squawk, and there was a pounding noise as one of the adults took wing, rising into the air. Flik and Karenk pressed themselves against the cliff, eyes wide. I dangled from the rope, unsure of what to do. Luckily, the pterodactyl flew off in the opposite direction. Taking a deep breath, I finished my climb. Once again, I was shaking and exhausted by the time I'd reached the top.

Crawling to the nest, I peered over the edge and saw that both adults were gone. I glanced into the distance and saw the one that had just left soaring out across the plain. Spotting me, the young pterodactyls screeched and jumped, tiny wings flapping uselessly. The yellowish-brown carcasses of their brothers and sisters lay scattered around them. Some had been partially eaten since my previous departure. I turned back to my companions and pointed at the adult pterodactyl in the distance.

"Grab some babies," I panted. "I'll get her attention."

I handed Karenk the reflective blanket. He and Flik stalked around inside the nest, trying to grab some of the crow-sized young. The squawking infants fought back, hopping out of reach and snapping at the kidnappers' outstretched fingers with their tiny beaks. Karenk managed to scoop up three of them, but earned a dozen scratches along his forearms as a result. Flik captured one, and received a bloody peck on his cheek. They fashioned a makeshift sack out of the reflective blanket and quickly stuffed the chicks inside. I stood up, shoulders apart, and drew a bead on the adult pterodactyl. I squeezed off a shot, intending to miss but attract the dinosaur's attention. Unfortunately, there was no discernable effect.

"Down the rope," I ordered. "Hurry!"

Karenk slung the bag over his shoulder, gripping it with one hand. Then he used his legs and free hand to propel himself down to the tunnel mouth. Flik started down next, pausing only to glance back at me.

"Hey," I shouted, cupping my hands over my mouth. "Hey, Mommy! Better come back to your nest!"

In the distance, the pterodactyl wheeled in mid-air. A terrible shriek echoed over the mountain. Then, she dropped and zoomed toward us. Her speed was incredible—much faster than I would have believed possible.

"Shit!"

Flik slid down the rope. I followed along, moving as quickly as I could. The rough texture of the rope burned my palms. When I reached the bottom, I saw that Karenk—obviously terrified—was about to climb back into the tunnel.

"No," I warned. "Wait! She has to see what we have. Flik, you start down instead."

A noise like a flying freight train hurtled toward us. The adult pterodactyl crashed down into the nest, splintering the twigs and branches. She perched on the edge of it, glaring at us. Although I could see no genitalia, I had no doubt this was the mother. It was something about her eyes and the fury they held. Her massive beak snapped open, revealing razor-sharp edges. Her foul breath wafted over us. She hissed, and then tilted her head, staring at the squirming bag.

"She sees it," I yelled. "Go, go, go!"

The baby pterodactyls did their job perfectly, squawking in fright as Karenk swung down into the tunnel. I scrambled for the rope as the parent roared, and then dropped toward us. She hit the ledge, talons skittering on stone and leathery wings stirring up dust, as I gripped the rope and slid. This time my palms didn't just burn. They were rubbed bloody. I lost my balance when I hit the bottom, landing on my butt. My teeth clamped together, and a jolt of pain shot through my already injured leg.

"Aaron?" Flik reached for me.

I waved him away. "Get back. I don't know if that thing can fit through the entrance or not."

The pterodactyl raged above us, blocking out the sunlight, and sending an avalanche of dirt and small stones tumbling down. The hatchlings screeched in response, further infuriating the beast. I stood slowly, testing my leg. It hurt, but luckily, I hadn't damaged it any worse and was able to put my full weight on it. Slowly, we backed away from the shaft. The dinosaur's fury was terrifying, but after a few minutes, I began to relax, realizing that she was too big to fit down the hole.

"Okay," I said. "Now comes the tricky part. We have to make our way back through the dark to the other entrance, and hope that she can hear her babies through all the rock and stone above us."

"And if she cannot?" Flik asked.

"Then we need to make these things scream when we reach the other side."

We turned toward the darkness and plodded ahead, going faster than we had before. While Flik and Karenk were certainly scared of our pursuer, they seemed to be less uneasy about the darkness than they had been on our first trip. We paused occasionally, listening for the pterodactyl. Karenk shook the reflective blanket, eliciting cries from the chicks, which in turn got a response from above, albeit muffled through the tons of stone between her and us. A few times we lost track of her—whether because she'd grown silent or whether the mountain had muted her, I do not know.

It occurred to me there in the darkness beneath the mountain that there was something I had overlooked. Why would the pterodactyl's hunt across the vast plain when they had this entire populace living just below their nest? Could it be that the Anunnaki were somehow poisonous to them, if eaten? Or did the snake men have some sort of defense that the pterodactyls were wary of? I fervently hoped that wasn't the case.

We rested only once, when we came across the astronaut's remains, and then only briefly. By the time we saw the dim sunlight ahead, signaling the tunnel exit, we were breathless and exhausted. My previous injuries ached, and the fresh wounds on my palms burned and throbbed. Even the mighty Karenk was tired. The babies, while unable to rip or tear through the heavy material of the reflective blanket, were not an easy or willing cargo, and their constant struggling had worn him down. I worried that the mother had grown tired, as well. The sounds of pursuit had faded for quite some time. Would that motherly instinct fade away? In truth, I suppose there was a part of me that hoped she had given up her chase. The unmitigated cruelty of what I was about to do was not lost on me. My stomach churned at the thought. But it had to be done. If

Kasheena and our people were to be saved, then others had to be sacrificed.

I ordered the two of them to stay back, and crept toward the tunnel exit by myself, frowning at the silence. I watched the sunlight on the ledge, looking for a wheeling shadow, but saw nothing. Slowly, I poked my head out and glanced upward. The sky was empty. I glanced back at Karenk and motioned at him to come forward. He did so nervously. I took the makeshift satchel from him, struggling with the shifting bulk. Then I pointed, indicating that I wanted him to go stand with Flik. Nodding, he complied.

"Be careful, Aaron," Flik whispered.

Shrugging, I tiptoed out into the sunlight. Tension marked my every step as I shuffled toward the edge of the ledge. I expected the mother to swoop silently down out of the sky and seize me at any second, but I think her absence disturbed me even more. When I reached the edge, I looked down on the city, half-expecting to see the occupants scurrying about, alerted to the chaos taking place far above them, but the Anunnaki seemed oblivious. I did notice that more of them seemed to be out in the courtyard than before, surrounding that giant pit. I quickly looked for our friends, but saw no sign of them. I hoped they were in place and just well-concealed, rather than delayed. Then I turned my attention back to the crowd standing around the edges of the pit. A human figure was among them, struggling. I squinted, trying to determine the person's identity, but the distance was too great. Whoever it was, their arms appeared to be bound behind them. One end of a length of rope had been tied around their waist. A phalanx of snake men forced him or her ahead with spear tips and swords. Then, as I watched, they began to lower the thrashing prisoner into the hole.

I glanced at the ridge above me. There was still no sign of the parent. Groaning with pain and exhaustion, I let the reflective blanket sag down onto the ledge and slowly opened it. Immediately, the imprisoned chicks began to squawk and shriek. Feeling a surge of remorse and guilt, I reminded myself that this was what needed to be done. These innocent newborns had to be sacrificed so that Kasheena and the others might live. Their shrill cries echoed over the rocky landscape, and were soon answered by a deeper, guttural croak that seemed to reverberate off the mountaintop. All at once there was a sound like an onrushing train. A shadow fell over me. Karenk and Flik shouted a warning. I looked up again, and saw the mother pterodactyl zipping toward me, talons outstretched. Her size seemed to blot out the sun.

Moving quickly, I snatched up two of the babies, ignoring the bites and scratches they delivered all across my hands and forearms as they struggled, and tossed them over the side of the ledge. Roaring, the mother veered in mid-flight, swooping out over the valley in pursuit of her hatchlings. When she started to turn back toward me again, I threw two more of the infants, making sure they cleared the canyon walls and fell straight toward the Anunnaki city. Tiny wings beat helplessly in the air as they plummeted downward. My bile rose at the sight, but I pressed on, committed to my atrocity, and threw two more. Their mother turned once more, choosing concern for her brood over revenge toward me, as I'd hoped, and rocketed after them. Taking advantage of her distraction, I grabbed the reflective blanket, dragged it to the edge of the ledge, and shook the remaining baby birds into the chasm. The eggs followed after, dropping like tiny anvils.

For some reason, at that moment, I remembered an old television show my father used to watch when I was a child, called *WKRP in Cincinnati*. In one episode, a radio station had arranged to drop live turkeys from an airplane as part of a Thanksgiving promotion. When the flightless birds had smashed into the city below, the beleaguered station manager had moaned, "As God is my witness, I thought turkeys could fly."

I giggled, thinking about that. Then my laughter turned to choked, remorseful sobs.

The adult pterodactyl, having forgotten all about me, descended upon the courtyard, intent upon her young. The helpless chicks hit the ground. Their mother's alarmed screeches echoed across the valley. Leaning out farther, I let the blanket go, and watched the sun shine off the reflective silver surface as it drifted down, billowing in the air.

"Come on you fuckers," I growled. "Come onnnnn ..."

I felt a surge of relief as the pterodactyl stormed the city. Mad with rage, she swept over the crowds, knocking snake men over and seizing victims in her claws. The Anunnaki scattered, running in every direction except the pit. A few unlucky ones who had been standing at the edges of the chasm, fell into the dark depths, arms pin-wheeling helplessly. Even now, as the crazed mother dinosaur began to rend and shred, they made no sound. There were no screams or cries of alarm. The only noise was that of the pterodactyl's fury. Then, it was answered by another cry from far above us.

I looked up and saw that the other adult—what I assumed was the father—had returned. It dived toward the city, talons flexing in anticipation of slaughter.

I turned back to my companions and motioned frantically. "Let's go! Hurry!"

Nodding, Karenk and Flik followed me back down the mountainside. Below us, new sounds echoed as the Anunnaki began to fight back. They still weren't screaming or crying out, but we heard gunshots and laser blasts and the clang of steel.

"Both of the parents," Karenk observed. "That is a good stroke of fortune for us."

Panting, I clambered over a boulder. "Let's just hope our luck holds."

"Aaron," Flik said, and then paused. His face was ashen. "What we just did..."

"We did it because we had no choice, Flik. If it makes you feel any better, I'm the one who tossed the babies over the side."

"But Karenk and I helped. We took them from their mother ... from their parents. We snatched them from their nest."

"And you did so because I told you to. This is on me, Flik. I'll carry the guilt. You just focus on the path, because if we don't get back down there and help our friends escape, then this was all for nothing."

# [ 12 ]
# ASSAULT ON THE ANUNNAKI

We descended into chaos. The mountain seemed to vibrate. The sounds of conflict boomed up from the city as we neared the ground. Weapons rang out and the pterodactyls shrieked and roared. For a brief moment, we heard something else—something we couldn't identify. It sounded like the hiss of a snake, but it had the tone and depth of a freight train. Unfortunately, the sound faded before we could discern what it was or where it had come from. Several explosions shook the boulders around us, dislodging smaller stones and debris. At one point, the air became thick with smoke, but that soon dissipated after we'd taken a few turns and descended further.

When Karenk, Flik, and I had embarked on our mission, I had tasked the others with positioning themselves under cover near the road, and rescuing the captives from the mud huts once we had provided the distraction with the pterodactyls. My hope had been that the Anunnaki would focus on the enraged pterodactyls, allowing our people time to escape. They were supposed to rendezvous with us at the encampment within the secret ravine Karune and I had explored earlier. If they couldn't reach the ravine, I'd told them to escape via the road, cross the stone plain, and meet us at the edge of the forest.

Upon arriving at the camp, Karenk, Flik and I were relieved to see that the rest of our party had indeed made it out of the city alive. Tolia, Ambrose, Trut, Karune, and Marta were accounted for, as was Fern. Upon seeing us, the baby triceratops bleated with excitement. Watching her made me think of the other newborn dinosaurs who I'd just flung to their deaths. Pushing the thought away, I stared at the throng accompanying our fellow rescuers, quickly estimating that there were a good fifty or sixty people packed into the ravine—men, women, and children, all of whom had been captured during the raid on our village. Both Karune's sister and child were safe, as was Tolia's son, Apotic. There were also a few strangers whom I didn't recognize. I assumed they must have been from other tribes and locations across the Lost Level and had also suffered imprisonment by the Anunnaki. Some of the freed prisoners were armed with weapons stolen from their captors. Others had only their fists and wits. A few seemed injured or ill. But there was one face missing among them. I clambered down and entered the milling crowd, frantically searching for Kasheena.

Now, you must remember, as you read this, I was not with them during the rescue attempt. I was busy causing the distraction. Perhaps you are disappointed that I can't give you a full accounting, but I simply was not there. I learned later, from the others, that there was indeed a fight, and that there were also casualties among both the captives and the Anunnaki. Ambrose also bragged with noticeable pride about how Fern had even joined the fray, charging through the snake men's ranks and knocking them over like bowling pins.

I continued slipping through the throng of people, looking for Kasheena. She was nowhere in sight.

"Ho, Aaron!" Ambrose made his way toward me, pushing

through the throng. Many of the new arrivals stared at him in confusion or curiosity. "I think it is fair to say your plan worked."

I nodded. "Have you seen Kasheena, Ambrose?"

"You must remember, my friend, I never met your lovely bride."

"Yes, but everyone else here has. You helped them rescue the captives. Was she among the prisoners?

The sudden change in his expression turned my stomach to knots. He wheezed, his asthma obviously aggravated from their escape.

"I believe you should speak with Tolia, Aaron."

"Why? Mr. Bierce, what's going on? Where's Kasheena?"

"Aaron ..." Chest heaving, Ambrose shook his head.

Panicked, I glanced around for Tolia and saw her approaching me. Apotic was with her, as was a man I didn't recognize. He was clad only in a dirty loincloth and his body was covered in crude black tattoos. He was armed only with a pointed stick. I ran to them.

"Tolia, what happened to Kasheena? Where is she?"

"Aaron, this is Patamoose." She gestured to the tattooed stranger. "He is from a tribe on the other side of the stone plain. He was among the prisoners."

"Nice to meet you." I nodded curtly and turned back to Tolia. "Tell me what's going on. Is she ... is she dead?"

"Kasheena is your woman?" Patamoose asked. His accent was thick, but surprisingly, he spoke the same language as our tribe.

"She is my partner," I said. "Do you know her?"

"I do. I was imprisoned with her. Had it not been for Kasheena, I would be dead now. All of us would. She gave us hope when there was none to be found. She kept us inspired—made us live."

"What happened to her?" I grasped his tattooed shoulder. "Did they kill her?"

Patamoose tilted his head from side to side, indicating uncertainty. "I cannot say she is dead. I only know what they did with her. There is a great hole in the center of the city."

"The pit. I've seen it."

The rest of the group began to gather around us, listening intently.

"A giant serpent dwells in the darkness at the bottom of that hole," Patamoose continued. "The serpent is longer than any tree, as big as any of the thunder lizards, and yet, the hole is so deep that it cannot climb free. It, too, is a prisoner of the dragon men."

I thought of the great hissing noise we had heard on our way back down the mountain, wondering if it could have been this snake he spoke of.

"Your people call them dragon men?" Trut asked. "Are you of the White Sand tribe?"

"I am." Patamoose nodded. "How do you know this?"

Trut grinned. "I spent some time with your people when I was a young man. Good folk. There was a girl—"

"Kasheena," I interrupted. "What does the hole have to do with her?"

"The dragon men worship the serpent as a god. They sacrifice some of the prisoners to it—lowering captives down on long ropes. They cut the ropes when the prisoner reaches the bottom. There is no escape from the pit. Kasheena was—"

"I saw her." I pounded my leg with my fist. "Goddamn it, I saw her earlier—saw them lowering somebody into the pit. But I was too far away. I couldn't tell ..."

The group began to talk all at once. Some of them expressed shock and dismay at Kasheena's fate. Others muttered in confusion. For a tribe who had no religion, other than the belief in a Creator who had made the Lost Level, it was puzzling to them why the Anunnaki would worship such a beast, and pay tribute to it with the blood of others.

"Snakes are often slow to eat their meal," Ambrose said.

I blanched at the thought.

He held up his hands. "All I am saying is that there may still be time, Aaron."

"Way ahead of you," I replied. Then I turned to the group. "Tolia, I want you to lead everyone back to the village. I will—"

"I am coming with you," she insisted. "I have known Kasheena since we were babies. I will not let this be her fate. Not while I am breathing."

"Bullshit," I countered. "You just got Apotic back, safe and sound. He already lost his father. I'll be damned if he's going to lose you, too."

"You listen to me, Aaron Pace—"

"No, you listen to me, Tolia. I know you love Kasheena. So do I. But she is all I have here. You have someone else. Don't let your thirst for revenge overwhelm your logic. You need to stay with Apotic."

She glanced down at her son. He hugged her waist and looked up at her with pleading, haunted eyes.

"You are right," Tolia said, looking back up at me. "It is not easy for me, but you are right."

Karenk stepped forward. "Then I will accompany you instead."

"Listen," I shouted. "I don't have time to argue with you people. You need to get everyone back to the village. It's going to take all of you to do that. All of you. Each of you has a skill. A worth. Think about what it took to get here. To get home, it's going to take Tolia's leadership, Karenk's strength, Trut's knowledge of the landscape, Karune's stealth, Flik's speed, and Marta's steadfastness. The tribe needs all of those things. The people back in the village need them even more. Our loved ones have been through enough already. Get them home safely—back to their families. Let Ambrose accompany you. Make him as welcome among our tribe as you made me. Fern, too."

They all stared at me. A few shuffled their feet, but no one spoke, and none other than Ambrose and Patamoose met my eyes.

Finally, Tolia said quietly, "We will do as you wish, Aaron."

"Okay," I said. "If there are no more arguments, somebody give me a sword."

Six blades were presented to me. I accepted Marta's. She performed a slight bow.

"Thank you for all you have done for our people, Aaron. I regret that I agreed with Apok when we started out. You are a good man. Apok was wrong. You are one of us."

"Thank you, Marta."

"Aaron ..." Ambrose stuck out his hand. "We said our farewells once before. I trust they still hold?"

I squeezed his sweaty palm. "They do. You'll be safe among my people, Mr. Bierce. And I think they can use you."

Nodding, he smiled. "I think I can use them, too, Aaron. Good luck. I pray you find her in time."

I bid them all a quick goodbye, certain that I would never see any of them again. When they didn't move, I urged them to flee and turned away. I heard several sobs behind me as I started along the ravine, but I did not turn around.

"Hang on, Kasheena," I whispered. "I'm coming ..."

After I'd gone a few hundred yards, I heard the faint, shuffling patter of bare feet on stone. Wheeling around, I saw Patamoose following along behind me, clutching his pointed stick defensively. His brow was furrowed.

"What are you doing?" I asked.

"I come to help you, Aaron Pace. My tribe is far from here, and I do not know how to find them again. I also do not know your people, but I know Kasheena and I know how desperate you are. If you will not accept my help, then kill me now."

Sighing, I shook my head. "You'll need more than that stick."

I yanked my combat knife from the makeshift sheath I'd fashioned from the blanket and handed the weapon to him. He appraised the blade with wonder.

"This is fine craftsmanship. I will accept it gladly. Although, you may be surprised what I can do with this stick."

"Come on." I turned. "Show me. And in case I don't get a chance later ... thank you."

The sounds of battle grew louder as we raced along the path, but I noticed that they weren't as frenzied now. Gripping the laser pistol in one hand and the sword in the other, I rushed ahead, anxious to reach the pit. Patamoose kept pace with me, despite being barefoot. I heard no complaints from him, even though the ravine was littered with sharp fragments of rocks. He must have had either incredibly thick calluses on his feet or a high tolerance for pain. We hurried in silence; not talking, saving our breath for the task ahead.

When we reached the edge of the city, I slid to a halt, gaping at the devastation. The courtyard was splattered with blood and body parts. The corpses of dead Anunnaki lay sprawled on the stones next to pulped baby pterodactyls. One of the adult pterodactyls also lay dead amidst the smashed ruins of a building. The creature's carcass was stuck full of arrows and still bled from hundreds of bullet holes. The other pterodactyl limped along, croaking in pain, dragging a broken wing behind it. A group of Anunnaki armed with clubs and swords tried to encircle the beast, but each time one of them got near, the dinosaur lashed out, hissing and slashing at them with its beak and talons. Further into the city, fires raged inside three of the towering spires. They reminded me of Roman candles. Flames and smoke belched from the windows, curling into the sky. As I watched, a panicked Anunnaki flung itself from the top of one of the buildings, desperately trying to escape the heat and smoke. The snake man hit the ground like a rotten pumpkin, splashing across the cobblestones. The streets were filled with running figures, but I saw no indication of organization or leadership. The city's inhabitants were operating on blind fear.

I'd be a liar if I didn't tell you the sight pleased me in a grim sort of way.

Grunting, I hefted my weapons and charged into the fray, leaping over mangled corpses and heading toward that massive, yawning hole in the ground. Patamoose ran along at my side, his expression one of ironclad determination. A snake man stood in front of us, his attention fixed on the fires. I slashed his throat without slowing my pace, killing the reptilian before he was even aware of our presence. Anunnaki blood arced across my face and shoulders. I spat it from my lips. Two other snake men charged toward us, thrusting with their spears, but Patamoose spun and parried, blocking their attack with his stick. The sound of wood striking wood rang out. Before I could draw a bead with my laser pistol, he'd tripped them both, sending them sprawling, and then finished both opponents quickly by plunging the sharp end of his stick into their eyes, driving the point into their reptilian brains. They jittered and then went limp. Patamoose placed one foot on the nearest reptilian's chest, and pulled his stick free with a wet, squelching sound.

"You're right," I panted. "I'm impressed."

"Here come more of them," he warned. "Get ready!"

The scattered hordes began to charge toward us. Although the Anunnaki raised no audible cry—at least none that we could hear—I had a sense that an alarm had been raised. We fought on, hacking and slashing and thrusting. I dropped three more opponents with the laser pistol, and perhaps a half-dozen more with my sword. My new companion did just as well. Despite having spent his recent time in captivity, Patamoose fought like a man possessed, showing no signs of weakness or fragility. He killed seven reptilians with just his stick, and another two with the combat knife. Once again, he appraised the weapon with clear delight, wiping the blood from the gleaming blade.

"I thank you again for this loan, Aaron."

"Keep it," I said. "You're better with it than I am."

We had almost reached the pit by the time the Anunnaki could muster any sort of organized response to our assault. They began to approach from all sides, armed with swords, axes, spears, and clubs. Only two of them had rifles, and another readied a longbow. I aimed for them first, even though they were furthest away from our location. While I sniped their riflemen, the rest of the Anunnaki pressed forward. Patamoose jumped up onto an overturned wheelbarrow and avoided a flurry of swinging blades. He kicked one reptilian in the face, pulping the creature's left eye socket beneath his heel. The snake man stumbled backward, making no sound, but clawing at its ruined face. Then it tumbled into one of its companions, sending them both sprawling. Patamoose speared the second one in the stomach before it could recover from the fall, and then back-flipped off the wheelbarrow, landing at my side. Back to back, we stood there panting, as the enemy closed ranks around us.

"You ready?" I asked.

He tossed his head, flicking the sweat from his brow, and grunted in affirmation.

The Anunnaki pressed forward. I counted twelve of them, with several more converging on us from across the courtyard. They had us surrounded on three sides. The only side open to us was the pit. It didn't take a brilliant tactician to know what they intended to do. They were going to try to force us backward, into the chasm. If we didn't go, then they'd kill us where we stood. I wondered how they would react if they knew that the bottom of the pit was our desired destination—albeit in one piece.

Silently, the Anunnaki charged. Patamoose spun his stick, deftly parrying several blows at once. He ducked low and a sword passed over his head. He gutted the attacker with his knife. Coils of intestine slipped down over the blade. I fired the laser pistol from my hip, sweeping the invisible beam from left to right. Six snake men fell back, mouths open in anguish, their scaly skin bubbling and blackening. I caught a whiff of roasting meat. To my horror, my mouth started to water. Two more foes shoved their blistering compatriots aside and charged at me with lances extended. I dropped flat on the ground, landing in a pool of blood, and lashed out with my sword, lopping off their feet. The blade caught in the second opponent's ankle bone, and I had to stand up to wrench it free. That was almost my undoing. A sword raked my side. Crying out, I recoiled, spinning to face the attacker, but Patamoose killed the reptilian before I could act, crushing the opponent's throat with two blows from his stick.

The last two stood facing us. Behind them, the other Anunnaki had slowed, gaping at the carnage we'd wrought. Then, slowly, they began to back away. I touched my side gingerly. My fingers grew slick with blood. Hurriedly examining the wound, I saw that it wasn't bad—nothing more than a scratch, really. Infection was certainly a possibility, especially if the Anunnaki had deliberately coated the blade with some sort of toxin, but I would have to worry about that later.

Patamoose's shoulders heaved as he gasped for breath. "You are hurt?"

I shook my head. "It's just a scratch. How about you?"

"One of them kicked my shin. That hurts. Otherwise, I am fine."

Across the plaza, the last pterodactyl cawed mournfully as a snake man thrust a spear into the dying creature's eye. The dinosaur shuddered, flapping about weakly, and then collapsed. It breathed once, twice—and then lay still.

"Come on." I hurried over to the edge of the pit. "We don't have much time. Without the pterodactyl to distract them, they'll be back on us with reinforcements in another minute."

"Ptero ...?"

"The dinosaur. We call it a pterodactyl."

"That is an odd name," Patamoose replied. "My people call it the Thunderbird."

Across the plaza, the Anunnaki were slowly regrouping, pointing and glancing in our direction. Then, they started to approach.

"We can discuss linguistics later, my friend."

Patamoose pointed. "There is the rope they used earlier. It is tied to yonder pole."

I picked up the frayed end of the rope and saw that it had been cut—or more likely sawed. It was made of thick, coarse fibers, and I had no doubt it would hold our weight. I just hoped it was long enough to reach the bottom. I tossed it over the side and watched it disappear into the blackened depths.

"Kasheena," I called, hand cupped alongside my mouth, "if you can hear me, hold on!"

There was no response from the darkness.

A great rumbling boomed across the valley and the stones shook beneath our feet as one of the towers collapsed. A cloud of dust and debris mushroomed into the streets and barreled across the city. Taking advantage of this new distraction, I stowed my laser pistol, wrapped my legs around the rope, and began to lower myself with my free hand. It was difficult to hold on. My palms were already raw from our climb down from the pterodactyl nest. I thought about dropping my sword and retrieving it once I'd reached the bottom, but if Kasheena was still alive down there, I couldn't risk it striking her.

"Can you do it?" Patamoose asked, peering down at me in concern.

"Yes," I grunted. "Just hurry up."

Patamoose hitched up his loincloth, secured the knife and stick within his waistband, and followed along after me. We inched down the rope, sunlight dwindling with every moment, until we were surrounded in darkness. I kept going, not looking down, listening to my breathing echo back to me, hearing my companion grunt above me. The void seemed to press against us. Soon, I couldn't even see the rope. When I looked up, Patamoose was just a gray smudge amid the blackness, and the sun seemed like a small copper coin. The air grew cooler, drying my sweat, and despite the heat baking off the landscape above, I shivered. The drafts grew stronger, bringing with them an odor. It reminded me of the Anunnaki—that cloying reptile house stench familiar to anyone who has ever visited a zoo. Grimacing, I opted to breathe through my mouth, but that just made it worse. I could taste the foulness at the back of my throat. The stench grew stronger the farther we descended. How far that was, I do not know. The darkness was complete now. I had no sense of movement, no idea how close we were to the bottom—if indeed there was a bottom. It occurred to me that this must be what it felt like to be an astronaut adrift in space. That, in turn, led me to think about Colonel MacKinnon and the revelations in his journal—a secret space program stretching all the way back to World War Two. He had mentioned the Nazi Bell. Kasheena, Bloop, and I had found a Nazi Bell shortly after my arrival in the Lost Level. Could there be a connection?

My arm began to ache, and then tremble. My legs felt like limp strands of spaghetti. The wound in my side still bled, and I began to wonder if I'd judged it incorrectly. Maybe it was more than a scratch. Maybe the Anunnaki had coated his blade with some sort of anticoagulant. That lizard stench grew stronger. The sword hung from my free hand, seeming as heavy as an anvil. Panting, I stopped my descent and dangled there, suspended over the void.

"Patamoose," I groaned, "stop for a moment."

"Are you in trouble?" His voice sounded so close, yet I couldn't see him.

Straining to hold on to the rope, I looked down into the darkness. "Kasheena? It's Aaron. If you are down there, stand against the wall!"

There was no answer, save my own echoes.

"Aaron," Patamoose asked, "what is the matter?"

"I need to lose my sword. If I don't, the weight is going to kill me."

I counted to ten, listening to my voice echo back up to me. Then I let go of the sword and grasped the rope with my other hand. Some of my trembling subsided, but I still felt weak and exhausted. The sword plummeted into the darkness, and although I waited, I did not hear it hit bottom.

"Okay," I said. "Let's keep going."

"Yes," he agreed. "My arms are turning numb."

My descent was made easier now that I had the full usage of both arms, but I still couldn't see where we were. Disoriented, I began to wonder if the pit was indeed bottomless? Perhaps Patamoose had been wrong about the monstrous serpent supposedly lurking in its depths. I glanced up again, hoping to see the sun, but now there was just a small sliver of light, no bigger than a firefly.

Suddenly, the rope began to vibrate and twist.

"Hey," I called. "Is that you, Patamoose? What are you doing?"

"It is not me," he replied. "I see figures above. I fear that the Anunnaki—"

The taught rope suddenly went slack in my hands. Someone had cut it far above us.

Then, a second later, I was falling into darkness again.

## [ 13 ]
## THE THING IN THE PIT

When I opened my eyes, there was light, orange and flickering, but surrounded by darkness on all sides. Just beneath it was Kasheena's face, never more beautiful, smiling down at me, her brown eyes wide and expressive.

"Oh, goddamn it ..." I sighed. "I'm dreaming again."

"Aaron?"

"Hi, baby." I tasted blood in my mouth, turned my head, and spat. Then I looked into her eyes. "It's good to see you. I just wish you were real."

Kasheena's brow furrowed. "I am no dream, and it is good to see you, too, my love. Now, unless you want this reunion to be short-lived, quit being lazy and get on your feet."

I blinked my eyes. "Kasheena? Is it really you?"

"Yes, Aaron. It is really me. Did you hit your head when you fell?"

I tried to move. My body ached, and the wound in my side felt like it was burning, but nothing seemed broken. Frowning, Kasheena stretched out one hand and I took it. A brief static shock passed between us. Then she helped me to my feet. We stared at each other for a moment. Then we fell together in a crushing embrace.

"I missed you," she whispered.

"I missed you, too. I thought ... I was afraid that ..."

"It is okay," Kasheena murmured. Her fingertips stroked the back of my scalp. "I have saved you. It is okay, now."

"Saved me? I was on my way to save you."

"And how did that work out for you?"

I interrupted her giggle by pressing my lips to hers. When we broke our kiss, Kasheena took a step back. I realized that the light was from a sputtering torch that she held in her other hand. Oily black smoke curled from it, drifting up toward the surface. I glanced behind me at the spot where I had landed and saw a pile of white and gray powder. Mixed in among the dust were various bones and skulls—animal, dinosaur, Anunnaki, human, and other types I couldn't identify. After staring at it for a moment, I realized that the powder was actually all that was left of what must have been an even bigger pile of bones at some earlier point in time. I looked for Patamoose amidst the debris, but saw no sign of him. Nor did I see the sword I'd dropped. The only thing I spotted, other than the bone dust, was the length of rope we'd been climbing down. I snatched it up and examined the end, confirming it had been cut. I checked myself over again, making sure I wasn't seriously hurt. My mouth was still bleeding. I'd bitten the inside of my cheek during the fall, but otherwise, I seemed okay.

The darkness here at the bottom of the pit was disconcerting. Far above, I saw a small circle of light, much like seeing the moon above. I knew that was the Lost Level's sun, but its light did not penetrate here.

I turned back to Kasheena. "There was someone with me."

She nodded. "Patamoose, yes. He is here."

"I fell on top of you." His voice echoed in the blackness beyond the torch. "You make a fine pillow, Aaron Pace."

A shadow, lighter than the darkness surrounding it, moved into the light. Patamoose smiled and nodded. He seemed uninjured, save for a shallow cut along his forehead. I clasped his hand and grinned.

"I am glad you're alive."

"And I am glad we found your beloved," he answered. "I found something, else, as well."

"Oh? What?"

He held up the sword and handed it to me. The torchlight glinted off the blade.

"Where's your stick?" I asked.

Patamoose sighed. "It did not survive the fall. It is broken into three useless pieces. But I still have the magical knife you gave me."

"It's not magical, Patamoose."

"It is to me, Aaron."

"Fair enough." I turned back to Kasheena and hugged her again. "How long have you been here? Are you okay? And where did you find that torch?"

She nodded. "I am fine. The torch was there. Amidst the bone dust. I do not know how long it has been down here, but it burns well."

"How did you manage to light it?"

Eyes glinting in the glow of the flame, Kasheena swept her arm to the side, extending the torch. Firelight flickered off a nearby stone wall that ringed the circumference of the pit. It stretched up into the darkness and was built from strange-colored rocks—gray and silver shot through with brick-red speckles. Each stone was roughly the size of a baseball. I recognized them right away. These rocks produced fire when ground together. Not a few singular sparks, like that produced from a piece of flint, but a flame like an arc-welder. I had first learned about them during my travels with Kasheena and Bloop, shortly after witnessing a battle between a Tyrannosaurus Rex and a giant weaponized robot. Our tribe held their value in high esteem, and they were incredibly difficult to find. Now, we were staring at hundreds of thousands of them. The pit's floor was just a smooth limestone slab, but the walls? The walls were an engineering marvel.

"Is the entire pit lined with these?" I asked.

Kasheena nodded. "Incredible, is it not? It must have taken generations to build."

"If we could figure out a way to pry them all loose and transport them, we'd be the richest people in the Lost Level. Did you find anything besides the torch in the pile of debris?"

"A few coins, some pieces of moldering cloth. Nothing else of value. Why?"

"I was thinking maybe we should search through the powder. Maybe we can find some more weapons or armor."

"We have more important concerns," Patamoose said. "Can you not smell it?"

I paused, and realized that I could. The bottom of the pit was dank and acrid, like the inside of a reptile house at a zoo. It stank of viscous intestinal matter and urine, and the cloying musk of a snake's cloacal glands. I cocked my head, listening, but the only sound was the three of us breathing, and the distant plink of water dripping somewhere.

"There's a snake," I whispered. "A big one. Kasheena, have you seen it?"

"No. After hearing the stories of this pit, I expected the serpent to set upon me as soon as I reached the bottom. But there has been no sign, other than that stench."

"We need to find a way out of here."

Kasheena laughed softly. "Oh, my love. I missed your gift for stating things that are obvious to all."

Patamoose chuckled quietly, hiding his mouth with his hands. His shoulders jostled up and down.

"I've got half a mind to leave you both here," I muttered.

"Then I would have to come rescue you again," Kasheena teased.

"Touché."

She frowned. "What does that mean—touché?"

"On my world, it's an acknowledgment that your opponent has scored a hit or a point."

"In my tribe," Patamoose said, "we have a similar word. Tooshy. It means the balls of shit that get caught in the fur around an animal's hindquarters."

"We call those dingle berries."

Kasheena's frown turned to disgust. "Berries? Your people eat them, Aaron? You should have told me this before all those times I kissed you."

"We don't eat them! It's a slang term." Seeing that she had no weapon, I held out my sword. "Here, you might need this."

"You keep it, Aaron. I have fire."

I shrugged. "Patamoose?"

"The knife will serve me well, Aaron."

"Okay." I nodded. "Let's find a way out of here."

We crept forward, sticking close to the wall. Kasheena took the lead, careful to keep her torch away from the stones. The last thing we needed was to accidentally catch the pit on fire and be roasted alive in the bottom of a massive underground oven. I was hesitant to use my laser pistol, should we need it, for the same reason. I followed a few paces behind Kasheena, clutching the sword in both hands. Patamoose brought up the rear. We could only see a few feet beyond the torch's glare. Everything else was enshrouded in darkness. The air was damp and still—no underground breezes or drafts of wind. Curiously, despite the lack of sunlight, the moisture, and our depth, the pit remained warm. I wondered what was heating it.

At one point, we came across a giant, waist-high mound of snake shit. Gagging, we were forced to leave the wall and head out into the blackness until we'd made our way around it again. A little further on, we encountered a massive, papery husk that filled all three of us with dread. It was the fragments of a shredded snakeskin, big enough to have been draped over a parade float. I had just knelt to examine it when we heard a monstrous hissing sound from somewhere on the other side of the pit. It was the same noise I'd heard during my descent down the mountainside, but much louder now. Indeed, the noise seemed to fill the pit, reverberating off the walls.

"It is coming." The confidence and bravery had vanished from Patamoose's tone. "What do we do?"

"Keep going," I urged. "Find a way out before it finds us!"

"But there is nothing," Patamoose gasped. "Just this endless circling wall!"

"Come on!"

We moved quickly, sacrificing stealth and silence for speed. I was pretty sure that between the torch and our own body heat, the serpent could track us anyway, no matter how quietly we moved. It was tempting to tell Kasheena to snuff out our light, but the thought of fumbling our way through that darkness with a giant predator hunting us was too much to bear. The hissing drew closer. Something moved in the darkness behind us. I heard a tremendous rustling sound—hide being dragged across the limestone floor. The snake smell grew stronger.

"Aaron! Kasheena! We have to stand and fight."

Patamoose stopped, turning to face the still unseen predator. A shadow loomed over top of us, momentarily blotting out the circle of light far above. It swayed back and forth, and the walls vibrated with the sounds it made.

Screaming, Kasheena clenched my arm. I glanced at her and then shrieked, as well. A second giant snake slithered toward us from her side.

"There's two of them," I shouted.

Instead of chiding me again for stating the obvious, Kasheena planted her feet firmly, shoulder-width apart, and waved the fiery torch at the second predator. The snake hesitated, nostril slits flared, eyes dilating as it followed the flame. I glanced back at Patamoose. The other snake paid no attention to the fire. It was focused on the warrior. The snake had probably meant to swallow him from above, before he could react. Now, it was unexpectedly faced with a foe who showed every indication of fighting back. Patamoose gripped the combat knife in his left hand, waiting for a strike. The snake glared at the weapon, and at its wielder.

"Aaron," Kasheena muttered, "I think I will use the sword after all."

I handed it to her, and drew my laser pistol from its makeshift holster, deciding it was better to risk a fire than to be swallowed alive by this abomination. Kasheena gripped the sword in one hand and continued to wave the torch back and forth with her other. Behind, us, I heard Patamoose breathe deeply.

"It's getting ready to—"

He grunted, pushing me backward and springing aside just as a snake head the size of a school bus darted downward. I caught a glimpse of a neck like a subway train. Then the slavering jaws closed on empty space. Patamoose rolled three times, positioning himself on his back just beneath the creature's neck, and stabbed upward with both hands. The blade parted scale and skin, sinking into the meat as easy as butter. I smelled rather than saw the blood. The snake reacted, spitting and hissing. It jerked its head skyward, thrashing in pain. Patamoose clung to the hilt with both hands, widening the gash before the knife slipped free of the wound. He tumbled back to the ground, and sprang to his feet.

Kasheena continued making long sweeping motions with the torch. The other snake remained focused on the flame, almost hypnotized. Slowly, Kasheena inched forward. She hefted the sword, and I saw what she intended to do. It took all my resolve not to cry out in alarm, but I refrained, not wanting to break the spell she had cast over the creature.

She tossed the torch to the side, toward the center of the pit. The fire arced through the air, leaving after-trails of light. The snake's eyes flicked to it, watching it go. Kasheena took advantage of the distraction and charged, leaping into the air with the sword hilt in both hands. She meant to drive the blade into the beast's head, just between its eyes.

The torch hit the ground, sputtered, and then went out, plunging us into darkness.

I summed up the situation with, "Shit."

Our foes could still see us, but we couldn't see them.

I sensed movement above us again, and felt a slight breeze ruffle my hair. The snake was there, lunging for a strike. I heard Patamoose breathing at my side, and knew he was clear. I raised the laser pistol and squeezed the trigger. The snake hissed, recoiling. I continued firing into the dark, making sure to aim above us.

"Stay down," I warned Patamoose.

A moment later, the wall sparked and glowed. One of my shots had struck it, igniting the fire stones. Flames sprang from rock to rock, blazing, filling the pit with light. The second snake reared back in surprise or fright. Patamoose cheered, raising his knife. I turned back to Kasheena and saw her riding atop the other snake's head, clinging to it like a rodeo rider on a bucking steer. Her legs were straddled across its broad skull, and she squeezed her knees tightly against it, trying to avoid being thrown off as it jerked and thrashed, whipping its head in a frenzy. The blade of the sword was buried in its skull, right between the eyes, but had only penetrated a few inches. Patamoose and I stood there gaping, watching with amazement as she pushed the sword deeper, inch by inch, straining with all her might. The snake let out one final, terrible hiss, and then it collapsed, tongue protruding from open jaws.

The other snake shuddered violently, and then began to thrash around. In its frenzied state, it smashed into the flaming wall, knocking loose several stones. The blazing debris tumbled to the floor, sending up a shower of sparks.

The fire raced along the wall, up and down and side to side. There was no smoke—only flame and heat, and already, that grew unbearable. Sweat poured off me as I glanced around, finally able to see the pit in its entirety. I stood there, stunned.

What we had mistaken for two snakes was actually one—a singular titanic monstrosity with two heads, one at each end. Its uncoiled length took up almost the entire far side of the chamber. It twisted and slithered spasmodically now, shuddering in its death throes. Its skin was black as night, and its belly was white. It occurred to me to wonder how it had been able to shit and piss, given that it seemingly had no tail end, but I wasn't about to get closer and examine the still thrashing corpse.

I spotted something else that filled me with dread. On the far side of the pit was a pile of broken egg shells, each one roughly five feet in circumference. All of them looked brittle and old. I wondered where the young had slithered off to. Had their parent eaten them, or had they escaped this chamber of horrors? Or worse, could they still be here, somewhere?

Kasheena climbed down from her perch, placed one foot against the snake's head, and yanked the sword free. She wiped the blade on the creature's hide, flicked her hair from her face, and glared at us.

"She is impressive," Patamoose muttered.

"Buddy," I whispered, "believe me. I thank my stars each and every night."

"As well you should, Aaron Pace."

"What now?" Kasheena yelled.

I scanned the pit, looking for a way out, but there was nothing. No tunnels or caverns leading into the mountain, no stairwells or ladders. The stones sparked and smoldered, bringing more flame and heat. The glare made it impossible to stare at the sides for too long. My lungs began to ache, and my pulse raced. It was getting hard to breathe. I realized that the fire was quickly depleting all of the oxygen in the pit.

"There," Patamoose shouted, pointing. "That fissure! Can we fit through it?"

Kasheena and I followed his gesture and saw a jagged crack in the limestone floor, about twenty feet away from us. The three of us hurried over to it. The fissure was about five feet long and maybe two feet wide. We couldn't see how deep it went or what was at the bottom.

"Should we try it?" I asked.

"We have no choice," Kasheena answered. "We will die if we stay here."

Nodding, I eased myself over the side, dangling my legs into the crevice. Then I slowly started to climb down, using whatever handholds and footholds I could find. Luckily, the fissure widened as it went deeper. I descended about fifteen feet, and found myself standing in a dark tunnel. I looked up at the others. I could see them, but they couldn't see me.

I cupped my hands around my mouth. "All clear!"

Patamoose climbed down next. When he'd regained his footing, I glanced up for Kasheena, but she was nowhere in sight.

"Where is she?" I asked, panicked.

"She said she had to get something."

"What?"

Before he could respond, the top of the fissure darkened. We looked up and, to my relief, saw Kasheena peering down at us. She held the sword in one hand. Her other hand had the torch, which she had recovered and reignited.

"Get out of the way," she shouted.

We moved back, and she dropped the torch down to us. I snatched it up and held it aloft, illuminating the tunnel. We were inside a natural cavern. It wasn't very wide or tall, but it was big enough that the three of us should be able to traverse it single file with some ease. Half-formed stalactites and stalagmites dotted the path, but I saw no signs of bats or other creatures—including the possible offspring of the two-headed monster above.

Kasheena quickly descended through the crack, and joined us at the bottom.

"Did you guys see those eggs up there?" I asked.

They both nodded. Patamoose shuddered.

"I pray we do not encounter any more like that," he said. "I nearly died from fright."

Above us, the pit began to rumble and shake. I glanced up, half expecting to see the snake burrowing toward us. Instead, I had to turn away, shielding my eyes from a sudden bright flare.

"The walls," Kasheena exclaimed. "I think they might be collapsing from the fire."

"Come on," I shouted. "This way!"

We darted down the tunnel, making our way around the obstacles, and hurrying to get clear. The path twisted and turned, sloping deeper into the underground. Soon enough, the rumbling sound increased behind us, becoming deafening. The cavern trembled, and we each grabbed on to the natural limestone pillars and columns to support ourselves and remain standing.

The pit collapsed, raining tons of burning stones down upon what was now the roof over our heads, and sealing the fissure.

“Well, we can’t get out that way,” I said. “And we can’t stay here.”

“We should rest,” Patamoose argued.

“Not here.” I shook my head. “With that opening sealed off, we don’t know if there’s another source of air down here. We could suffocate to death. We’ve got to keep moving.”

“You have the torch,” Kasheena murmured. “Lead on.”

## [ 14 ]
## BENEATH THE LOST LEVEL

I don't know how long we journeyed, with only the light from our flickering torch. Eventually, it started to fade and weaken, and we quickly fashioned another one using my frayed pants legs. I had come to the Lost Level wearing a pair of denim jeans. Now, they were nothing more than a pair of dirty, threadbare cutoff shorts. Soon, I would have no choice but to wear the same garments as the rest of our tribe.

Patamoose was terrified of the dark. He fought hard to conceal it from us, but I knew just the same. Like most of the Lost Level's denizens, he had known perpetual sunlight his entire life and was unaccustomed to this all-encompassing darkness. He walked between Kasheena and me. I let him carry the torch, and that seemed to alleviate his fears somewhat. When he spoke, it was only in whispers, and his hands trembled.

The passageway didn't widen, and there were no offshoots or other tunnels—at least, none that were big enough for us to fit through. The cave continued to slope steadily downward, taking us deeper and deeper. Eventually, the tunnel opened into a wide alcove. It was there that we decided to rest. We found a small, shallow pool of water in the center of the chamber. After examining it to verify the liquid was safe—there is an amoeba-like creature in the Lost Level that looks like a pool of water—all three of us drank greedily.

Kasheena and I climbed up onto a ledge about ten feet off the ground. It jutted from the wall, wide enough that we could lay down side-by-side without fear of rolling off in our sleep.

"I will stand first watch," Patamoose called up from below.

I leaned out over the ledge. "Are you sure?"

He smiled, his features lit by the torchlight. "I am certain, Aaron. The two of you should have time to do as all lovers do. I will stand guard and make sure the flame does not die. I wish we could start a campfire, but we have no fuel."

Nodding, I tossed down my other pants leg. "Use that if the torch starts to go out."

He nodded back at me, and then turned away, hunkered over the torch. I felt a surge of pity for him, this new friend, born here in the Lost Level, and yet, still so far from home and those he loved. He reminded me of Bloop in a way. My spirits fell.

"What are you thinking about, Aaron?" Kasheena asked.

I shrugged. "Home. Not my home, but our home. The village. I'm thinking about all the people we lost."

"The Anunnaki will not bother us again. This was the last time. They have been defeated."

"Have they? I'm not so sure. Their city is in ruins, but what if they have more? Or what if it extended underground? What if this tunnel is leading us directly to them?"

"If so, then we will face them together, my love."

"And what? Kill each and every last one of them?"

"Aye." She nodded. "That is exactly what we will do."

"Those are some long odds."

"We have faced all sorts of dangers together, Aaron. I care not, as long as you are with me."

I nodded, but remained silent. After a moment, she nudged me with her elbow.

"What troubles you, my love?"

"I don't want to lose you again, Kasheena."

"Nor I you."

Then Kasheena reached out to me, and pulled me into the darkness, and we made some light of our own.

---

EVEN NOW, all these years later, I think back on that moment and I smile.

I weep and I smile.

I would write more, but I have reached the end of this accounting ledger. The next part of the story—what we found there, beneath the Lost Level, and how it tied in with the map and the giant sword—will have to wait for another time. Outside this office building, the desert winds have begun to blow and howl, whipping up the sand. The tiny grains scrape against the building, and the sound reminds me of that two-headed snake in the pit.

I'm glad I found this shelter. There is going to be one hell of a storm.

I sit here, not afraid, but alone.

Old and alone, and so very far from home.

# AUTHOR'S NOTE

Some of the dialogue of the fictional Ambrose Bierce, who appears in this story, has been taken and repurposed from interviews with and quotes from the real-life Ambrose Bierce. This material has been repurposed under Fair Use, and no infringement or disrespect of the original work is intended.

# AFTERWORD

And so ends the second book in *The Lost Level* series. Thanks for buying it. I hope that you enjoyed reading it as much as I enjoyed writing it.

The next book to follow in this series, *Hole in the World,* will actually serve as a prequel of sorts. It takes place in a different part of the Lost Level, and features a different cast of characters, all of whom arrived in this lost dimension before Aaron Pace. Despite that, it ties into this novel, and the previous novel, as well. (In advance of any complaints this might incur, I'd just like to point out that Edgar Rice Burroughs did the same thing with his *Pellucidar* series—of which *The Lost Level* owes a great deal of inspiration. Early *Pellucidar* novels focused on main protagonist David Innes. Later novels didn't include Innes at all, or only for a cameo, and instead were centered around cavemen, Tarzan, and other explorers).

The fourth book in the series, *Beneath the Lost Level,* will pick up where we just left off, with Aaron and Kasheena and their new friend Patamoose, as they explore the underground caverns and ... well, I don't want to spoil it for you. Suffice to say, I'll let you see it as soon as I am done writing it.

Readers often ask me how long this series will be. The truth is, I don't know for sure. I've just outlined the next two books above, and I have ideas for at least three or four more novels to follow those. So, I guess this series could keep going for a while, as long as readers keep supporting it. I do know that Aaron's story has a definitive end, and I know what that ending is, but he has many other adventures to recall before we get to that point.

What follows now is a special bonus—a short story called "The Chinese Beetle." It features Aaron and Kasheena and takes place between *The Lost Level* and the novel you just read. It was previously published only as a rare, signed, limited edition chapbook. I offer it now for everyone to enjoy.

I'll see you all back here for *Hole in the World* and *Beneath the Lost Level*. Don't get lost on the way ...

Brian Keene
Somewhere along the Susquehanna River
December 2016

# THE CHINESE BEETLE

My name is Aaron Pace, and I'm writing this by hand on some loose sheets of printer paper I found inside of a plastic storage container—one of those supposedly airtight, waterproof type that people use for moving their belongings or to store Christmas decorations in. The paper wasn't the only thing I found inside the container, either. There was also a coffee mug emblazoned with the logo for *Leatherface: The Texas Chainsaw Massacre III*, a half-dozen ballpoint pens, a paperback western novel written by someone named Oliver Lowenbruck, and twelve issues of a newsletter called *The Black Lagoon Bugle*. The book is missing its front cover, but beggars can't be choosers, and good reading material—or even bad reading material—is hard to come by in this place. As for the newsletters, each issue is printed on some of the ugliest paper I've ever seen—dark green, lime, blue, teal, and a shade I can only describe as salmon. That last is the same color of the papers I'm writing this on, and I apologize in advance for that.

The newsletters are all dated from 1991 to 1994, and targeted at enthusiasts, fans, and memorabilia collectors of the film *The Creature from the Black Lagoon*. On the last page, there's a Los Angeles address listed for correspondence and subscriptions. Despite all of that, I know these back issues aren't from my world—my reality—because they mention that the actor playing the titular Creature was named Max Samuels. On my Earth, the Creature was played by two actors—Ben Chapman and Ricou Browning.

That's one of the problems with the Lost Level. You might stumble across something here that looks familiar, only to discover it's not what you thought it was, or it's not from where you thought it would be. It's like getting a letter from home, only to find out it's written by someone you don't know and addressed to a stranger.

That's what this dimension is called—the Lost Level. If you've found the other journal I left behind (in the back of a school bus), then you already know that. If not—if you're new here—then perhaps a brief explanation is in order. I'll have to keep it short, though, because there aren't many of these blank sheets.

I came to the Lost Level by accident, via something called the Labyrinth, which is best described as an interdimensional pathway of energy running through space and time. The Labyrinth touches and connects everything in our universe. Since all the planets, stars, and galaxies are connected together by the Labyrinth, those who know how can use it to travel from planet to planet and star system to star system. But they can also travel to other dimensions and alternate realities. These other-dimensional realities are often referred to as "levels." But there is one level that is different—a dimensional reality that exists apart from the others, a place where the flotsam and jetsam of space and time washes up from across the shores of the multiverse. That place is called the Lost Level, and if you are reading this, then you are in it, and you can't leave.

I had been using an occult ritual to explore alternate realities.

Ultimately, that led to my being trapped here. One moment I was at home in Wisconsin, and the next, I was stranded here.

Soon after my arrival, I made friends with two other inhabitants. The first was Bloop, a strange, blue-furred cross between a cat and an ape, who was as brave and agile and loyal companion as one could ever hope to have. The other was Kasheena, the warrior princess of a local tribe, a ferocious and valiant fighter whose wits, cunning, and skill with a sword were matched only by her beauty.

We journeyed together to Kasheena's village. It was a long trip, made longer by the fact that it is impossible to mark the passage of time here in the Lost Level because the sun never sets. It simply hangs in the sky, providing light and illumination, the way all suns do, but it is motionless. Kasheena saved my life numerous times during that journey. Indeed, most of the survival skills I've learned here came from her. Eventually, we reached her people, but at a terrible cost.

I settled in among Kasheena's people, making a life for myself in the village. I grew close to her father, and to Shameal, the tribe's wise-man. Some of the tribe members were distrustful of me at first, but in time, I began to win them over. One of the ways I accomplished that was through hunting. And it was during a hunting trip that Kasheena and I encountered what I came to think of as the Chinese Beetle.

The immediate area surrounding the village is mostly farmland, which the villagers utilize with amazing proficiency. Past the tended fields are wide open plains, dotted here and there with bushes and scrub trees and occasional, thin pockets of woodland. Eventually, the plains become covered with tall grass. Beyond this are vast swaths of forest and jungle.

Kasheena and I were in the grasslands, about a mile from the edge of a forest, hunting wild game. We had little to show for our efforts, except for two rabbits (one much like the kind back on

Earth and the other with a long, curled tail and shorter ears), and a buzzard-like bird that Kasheena called a Klektick. I thought the latter looked pretty unsavory, but she promised me it would taste perfectly fine, provided we removed all of the fat from the meat before cooking it.

"The Klektick is a scavenger," she explained. "It tastes like whatever it eats, and it stores that taste in its fat."

I'd heard hunters and fishermen back home say the same thing about bears and carp, so I had no reason to doubt her, but I was still dubious, and let her carry the ugly bird in her game bag. I kept the rabbits in mine. We'd already field-dressed the animals. Both of our bags were fashioned from tanned hides. We were each armed with bows and quivers of arrows, although Kasheena's marksmanship with a bow was far superior to mine. We also had knives sheathed at our waists. In addition, I had my sword with me. The only other thing we carried with us was water. We didn't bring rations, as we'd planned on being back in the village before it was time to sleep. As we moved slowly through the tall grass, I lamented not bringing my pistol. I'd left it behind because ammunition was scarce, and I had no means to reload my bullets. It was better to save what little remained for a day when I might need it, rather than wasting it on a hunting trip.

We refrained from talking, focusing instead on staying quiet, lest we scare away any potential game. But it didn't really seem to matter, as wildlife was oddly scarce that day. The only movement was the grass itself, swaying slowly back and forth in the slight breeze.

"This is futile." Kasheena pouted, beads of sweat shining on her upper lip. "We should make our way back, Aaron. Perhaps one of the other hunting parties has had better luck."

"Let's go a little further," I urged. "At least as far as the tree line. Maybe it's the heat. We might find some animals in the forest, where it's cooler. And to be honest, I could use a little shade myself. What little breeze we have out here isn't doing much."

Kasheena conceded to my plan and we headed on, walking side by side, parting the grass with our bows. I reached out and took her hand, and gave it a squeeze. Smiling, she returned the gesture. We pushed ahead, and emerged into an area where the grass had been crushed and flattened.

And that was when we found the tracks and stopped dead in our own.

"What did this?" Kasheena asked. "I have never seen tracks like these."

Two deep ruts had been gouged into the dirt, chewing up the topsoil on either side of them, and squashing the vegetation. The spacing was about the width of a small car. They looked like tank treads, and I said as much.

"It looks like a tank rolled through here."

Kasheena let go of my hand. "A tank?"

"Remember the airplanes we found?" I was referring to five TBM Avenger torpedo bombers we had discovered about a month earlier. "Tanks are something similar—a mechanized vehicular weapon of war."

"Do these tanks fly as well?"

"No ... at least, not during my time. But depending on what time period it came from before arriving here?" I shrugged. "Anything is possible."

"I would suggest this tank did not fly." Kasheena pointed at the ground. "Judging by the tracks. Although, I do not understand what happened to it."

The trail led off toward the forest, but seemed to start abruptly from where we stood, right in the middle of the grassland. Kasheena was perplexed by this, but I knew right away what had occurred. Whatever the identity of the machine—a tank or some other type of all-terrain vehicle—that had left these marks, it had materialized out here in the middle of the grasslands. Like myself, the machine and its crew were probably dimensional castaways, caught up in the current of the universe and deposited here in the Lost Level. There was little doubt in my mind that they had emerged on this spot, and then the driver had headed for the tree line, perhaps seeking cover. Shielding my eyes with one hand, I peered at the forest, hoping to catch a glimpse of movement or the sunlight reflecting off metal, but the horizon was vacant.

"Could it present a threat to our people?" Kasheena asked.

I shrugged. "I guess so. It really depends on the intentions of its crew, though. We wouldn't really know until we found them. But yes, it unnerves me that it's this close to the village. Should we investigate?"

"I think we must. I also think I want more time alone with you before we go back."

"I like the way you think."

Kasheena smiled. "Do not worry, Aaron. If the people in this tank are hostile, I will protect you."

"Oh, I have no doubt." I grinned. "You're good at that."

Dispensing with any further attempts at hunting, we followed the tread marks across the grassland. The sun beat down on us mercilessly, but there was a light, steady breeze to counteract it—not enough to cool us, certainly, but enough to keep us from sweating and make the grass sway.

As we trailed our quarry, I noticed something odd. At certain points during its trek, it appeared as if the tank had stopped. Perhaps even stranger, there were signs that the tank—or the crew inside—had interacted with the environment. At one such location, a twelve-inch square of topsoil had been neatly excised from the ground. At another, there was a series of foot-deep bore holes in the dirt, each one about six inches in circumference. At a third location, it looked like the vegetation had been plucked from the earth, roots and all. After this, I began to pay closer attention to the ground, rather than the tracks themselves, and noticed a few spots where it looked like stones and rocks had been removed, leaving behind bare indentations. Whoever—or whatever—we were pursuing, they were collecting samples of the topography. But for what purpose?

Early on, shortly after I first arrived in the Lost Level, Kasheena, Bloop, and I had an encounter with what I can only describe as aliens. They were just like the ones portrayed in the media back on Earth—short, slender, gray-skinned beings with big oval eyes and a slit for a mouth. We escaped from them, thanks to Bloop, and I hadn't seen any since then. Of course, now I am much older, and have been here so long, and I have encountered them many times since. But on the day we found the Chinese beetle, I'd just had that lone encounter. Indeed, so many other bizarre things had happened to me since, so many oddities, that I'd nearly forgotten it.

Now, standing there in the tall grass, I mulled it over again, wondering if these tank-like tracks we were following might be associated with them. The modern mythology built around aliens always involved them collecting samples of things—stories of cattle mutilation and the harvesting of sperm and tissue from human abductees. Could something similar be at work here?

The trees at the edge of the forest cast a long shadow over us, as we reached the end of the grassland. The vegetation was slimmer in that shade, due to the fact that the sun never moved. It felt good to stand in it, though, and we did so for several minutes, enjoying a respite from the constant sunlight. The tank tracks disappeared into the tree line and the shadows grew deeper there.

"The forest is quiet," Kasheena observed, her voice barely above a whisper.

I nodded. Quiet was an understatement. The silence was

unnerving. There should have been birds chirping, animals scurrying through the undergrowth or skittering along the treetops. But instead, there was nothing. Even the insects seemed to be missing. It was as if the forest was afraid.

If so, then it was easy to see why. Our mysterious quarry had carved a trail of destruction through the dense vegetation, pulping ferns and wildflowers, and flattening small saplings. The ruts turned and weaved around the bigger trees, which indicated to me that the object was being piloted by some sort of intelligence. Kasheena and I glanced at each other, nodded, and then stepped into the gloom. We'd only gone a few yards into the forest when I noticed more signs of sample collecting. Bark had been sheared from several different trees, and there were bore holes in the trunk of two others. I paused to inspect them. The incisions were precise and geometrical. There were signs of digging in the forest floor, as well, and areas where the leaves and other detritus were swept away, exposing bare dirt and roots.

After another hundred yards, we came across a large, red boulder—a type of stone I'd never seen on Earth—that had very clearly had a section of it chiseled off. Scoring from some sort of tool was apparent on its surface and fragmented splinters of rock and dust lay around its base, covering the fallen leaves and other detritus. Kasheena knelt, picked up a handful of dust, and let it sift through her fingers.

"Why is this tank attacking the rocks and trees?" she asked. "Does it think they are enemies?"

"I can't be sure, but I suspect that someone is collecting samples of everything."

"But why?"

Before I could respond, the silence was broken by a grinding noise—the sound of metal on metal, like transmission gears slipping in an automobile. Kasheena leapt to her feet and readied her bow, notching an arrow in the time it took me to cast aside my own bow and draw my sword instead. The noise echoed through the forest, then came again.

"It sounds like it is in a great deal of pain," Kasheena whispered.

I pointed with my sword in the direction of the sound. Not surprisingly, it was the same direction as the tracks. We crept forward, our nerves on edge. Kasheena was usually unflappable. Her response to danger was usually either anger or grim resolve. But now her expression and posture hinted at fear.

The grinding continued, followed by a pop and sputter. Then silence descended on the forest once again. Kasheena stared at me, wide-eyed. I realized that I was holding my breath. Just as I exhaled, a new sound started—hydraulics. They hummed, ramping up in both speed and volume. Then, the forest began to rumble as what sounded like a bulldozer began coming toward us. The undergrowth swayed and shook. Saplings toppled over. Kasheena and I jumped behind trees on either side of the tread marks as the thing emerged into view.

I hadn't been far off the mark in calling it a tank, because the machine did indeed have tank-like treads propelling it across the ground. But that was where the similarities ended. Its size and shape reminded me of a Volkswagen Beetle, but this was no car. The metal hull was silver and black, and a number of devices protruded from it. Two tiny satellite dishes, about the size of frying pans, rotated on its top, and its sides were lined with various sensors and lights. Four mechanical arms stuck out from the sides. Each arm was equipped with a different type of tool, one of which was a sort of chainsaw, but with teeth that looked designed to cut through stone, rather than wood. I spotted some recessed panels and slots, where I suspected other arms were located. There was Chinese lettering on the side of the hull. I don't read or speak Chinese, so I have no idea what it said, but I'll do my best to reproduce the characters here, from memory.

国家航天局
火星探测探头

There was no windshield or view screen or windows of any kind, nothing to indicate that the vehicle was occupied, or even operated, by a living being, but of course, I couldn't be sure. It certainly moved like it was being piloted by some form of intelligence, weaving around the bigger trees and obstacles without pause. Perhaps most astonishing was the thing's speed. It burst from the foliage and raced toward our location. The hydraulics hummed and the treads clanked. The sound reminded me of the old wooden roller coasters I used to ride when I was a kid.

I motioned at Kasheena, indicating to her that we should stay hidden, and pressed myself up against the tree trunk, hoping that the mechanical monster would race past us and back out into the grasslands.

Instead, it stopped right next to us, in between the two trees. With a hiss, a hatch opened in the side of the hull and a thin, automated tentacle—barely the width of a pencil—extended from the beetle's interior. I caught a glimpse of circuitry and hydraulic lines inside the machine. It was then that I realized this was a robot. There was no crew inside. Instead, it was being guided by a computer. The beetle had to be a probe of some kind, perhaps for space exploration or search and rescue operations.

The metal tendril raised itself to my height and swiveled back and forth like a snake. There was a small blue light at its tip. Staring into it hurt my head. The arm paused in front of my face. Before I could react, the light flashed, and then the tentacle retracted back into the machine. Spots danced before my eyes. I realized that I'd just had my picture taken.

Kasheena, thinking I was being attacked, sprang into action. She unleashed an arrow, but it snapped on the beetle's metal hull. She quickly pulled another arrow from her quiver, notched it, and fired at a different spot, getting the same result. Without pausing, she tossed her bow aside and charged toward the thing, preparing to leap atop it. Before she could, one of the larger mechanical arms swung toward her, knocking her aside. With a grunt, Kasheena fell to the ground, sprawling in the leaves. Her arrows spilled out all around her, and the skinned and field-dressed Klektick fell out of her game bag. One of the probe's arms swiveled down to investigate it.

"Kasheena!"

She raised her head, looking dazed. I saw blood trickling from the corner of her mouth and a red welt just below her breasts.

Enraged, I swung my sword. It was an emotional, reactionary attack. Had I stopped to think for a second, I would have realized the futility of such an action. But I didn't think. I saw the woman I loved bleeding, and I responded in kind. My blade struck the hull with a clang. Sparks flew. The shock of the blow reverberated up my arms, momentarily numbing my hands, and I had to struggle just to retain my grip on the hilt of my weapon. The sword left a scratch on the probe's steel hull, but otherwise didn't seem to affect it. The beetle responded to my strike with a flurry of movement. One robotic arm, equipped with a pair of pincers, seized my blade. A second pincer-equipped arm, longer and narrower than the first, latched onto my hair, pulling tight. A third arm – the one with the chainsaw at the end of it – swiveled toward me, buzzing furiously.

The tank snatched the sword from my grip as easily as a bully taking a lollipop from a small child. It dropped the sword out of my reach. I struggled to free myself, twisting back and forth, as the spinning blade drew closer and closer. Sunlight glinted off the sharp metal teeth. I reached above my head with both hands and grabbed the appendage clenching my hair, trying to break its grip, but to no avail. The chainsaw was only inches from me now, and seemed to dominate my vision. The sawblade blocked out the sun and trees. The smell of scorched metal seemed to envelop me.

Gritting my teeth, I took a deep breath and flung myself backward, throwing all of my weight into the effort. I hung there, dangling by my hair for a second, but then the roots tore free from my scalp. The agony was unbearable. It felt like my head was on fire, but my escape attempt worked. I crashed onto the forest floor, gasping in pain. Above me, a chunk of my hair dangled from the robot arm.

The tank paused for a second, as if recalibrating. Then it changed direction, turning toward me, and trundled forward. I crab-walked backward, wincing as rocks and thorns dug into my palms. The probe rolled after me, relentless. I tried to scurry out of reach, but another of those damned arms seized my ankle. The pincers squeezed, and I screamed again, feeling the bones in my foot grind together. As if in response, the pressure subsided somewhat. The beetle didn't let go, but it didn't break my ankle, either. It seemed to be waiting for something, or perhaps studying me, pausing to gauge my reaction. Then, it released my foot.

"Thank you," I said.

If the robot understood me, it didn't respond. Then I remembered the Chinese writing on its side and decided to use one of the few Chinese phrases I knew, half remembered from a movie I'd once seen.

"*Xie xie.*"

The high-pitched hydraulic sounds seemed to decrease. I moved my legs, and when that got no violent reaction, I got to my feet with careful, exaggerated slowness.

"So, you can understand me?"

The probe simply hummed and whirred.

Suddenly, Kasheena clambered up onto the beetle's roof. Her expression was savage. She had cast aside her bow and instead clutched a football-sized rock, which she immediately used to batter one of the small satellite dishes that was spinning round and round. She struck it three times in rapid succession before our foe could react, bending the dish and arresting its rotation. As the probe's arms swiveled toward her, Kasheena smacked the dish again. The device snapped free, dangling off the side, connected only by a series of cables. I was momentarily hopeful that the damage might slow the robot or render it immobile, but there was no noticeable reaction. Instead, two more tentacles emerged from either side of the hull and swung toward Kasheena.

I shouted at her to jump, but she was already ahead of me, leaping up and latching on to a low-hanging tree limb. Agile as a cat, Kasheena swung herself up into the branches and then dropped down on the other side of the probe, landing at my side.

The probe thrummed.

I snatched up my sword and grabbed Kasheena's arm. "Run!"

We darted around the robot as its arms flailed and thrashed. The treads clanked as it began to pivot. Then it rumbled toward us. Obviously, the probe's artificial intelligence now saw us as a threat. I charged toward the edge of the forest, pulling Kasheena along behind me.

"Aaron!" She shook free of my grip. "We cannot lead it toward the village. We must go deeper into the forest. The trees and obstacles might slow it down."

I nodded. "Good thinking."

She led us to the right, far out of reach of the probe's various appendages, and then turned, heading into the trees. The beetle rolled after us. We ran from side to side, trying to further confuse our pursuer and slow it down. Vines and thorns tore at us as we plowed into the undergrowth, and low-hanging branches whipped our skin. The probe crashed through these obstacles without slowing. My foot caught a root sticking up from the soil and I stumbled. Had Kasheena not reached out and caught my arm, steadying me, I'd have probably been crushed beneath the robot's tank treads.

Kasheena led us on, darting around trees and leaping over logs and rocks. It was an effective method. I risked a glance over my shoulder and saw that although the probe was still doggedly pursuing us, its speed had slowed as it tried to navigate around the obstacles.

Eventually, the undergrowth began to clear, but we found a swift-running stream and splashed across that. The banks were strewn with slippery, slime-covered boulders and the water was knee-deep. The ground on the far side of the creek sloped upward at a steep incline. I saw a bed of light green ferns at the summit. Most of the fronds were taller than we were. We climbed the hill, grabbing onto saplings to keep our balance. When we reached the top, we paused, glancing behind us and gasping for breath.

The beetle slowed to a crawl as it reached the stream. It stopped for a moment, surveying the landscape, and then trundled into the water. It made another one of those horrible grinding sounds as the creek flowed over its treads, but it pushed on and emerged on the other side, cumbrously navigating between two boulders.

I heard something croak from inside the ferns, but paid it no mind. I was too focused on the probe.

"Can tanks climb hills?" Kasheena asked, breathless.

I wiped my forehead with the back of my hand. "I think we're going to find out."

But I was wrong. We never did get to find out because at that moment, something rustled in the ferns behind us. The croaking sound was repeated, but it was louder this time—more urgent. It was followed by a series of tiny, frightened trills. Kasheena and I glanced at each other in alarm. Something snorted loudly. Slowly, I parted the ferns with my sword.

We found ourselves staring into the face of a mother triceratops. Two frightened babies hid behind her back legs. The ground and vegetation around them was squashed flat, and littered with the fragments of egg shells.

The mother snorted again, louder this time.

"It's a nest ..."

With a throaty roar, the triceratops charged us, sweeping through the ferns with its massive head, horns whistling as they slashed the air. Kasheena leapt to one side, avoiding the onrushing beast. I wasn't nearly as nimble. I tumbled backward, arms pin-wheeling, and fell down the hill. I cried out in pain, trying to tuck myself into a ball as I rolled uncontrollably. Rocks sliced my skin, and my knees and elbows slammed against stones and logs. I reached and snagged a sapling, but only managed to yank it out of the ground. I only stopped when I reached the bottom, and by then, I was so stunned and in so much pain that I could only lay there, gaping.

The dinosaur galloped down the hillside after me, its hooves thundering on the rocks. The beetle thrummed and buzzed, clanking slowly up the slope. The arm with the camera on the end swiveled forward and snapped a picture of the charging beast. The flash of light further enraged the triceratops, who completely ignored me and focused instead on this new threat.

Flesh and horn met silver and black steel with a tremendous crash. Incredibly, the triceratops's horns accomplished what my sword and Kasheena's arrows had been unable to do. They pierced the beetle's hull. The probe shuddered and groaned, and the grinding noise returned again, louder than ever. This time, it didn't abate. The robot attempted to use its chainsaw, but the automated arm seemed to freeze in mid-swing, as if it had locked up. The sawblade sputtered and slowed.

The triceratops dug her feet into the soil and shoved with her head. The probe's treads spun, kicking up dirt and rocks. The two pushed each other back and forth, neither gaining much headway. Oily black smoke curled out from around the dinosaur's horns. Groaning, the enraged mother jerked her horns free, leaving three massive holes in the beetle's side. More black smoke belched from these, and I saw sparks flashing inside.

"Aaron!"

I sat up, wincing, and spotted Kasheena beckoning to me.

"Hurry, Aaron. This way!"

Slowly, I tried to stand, but the pain was too severe and my vision blurred. Instead, I crawled toward her. Something warm and wet stung my eyes. I blinked, wiping it away. When I looked at my palm, I saw blood.

The triceratops lowered her head and charged the beetle again. The probe responded by slapping her with one of its tentacle arms. The dinosaur shook her head, snorting in surprise and then renewed her attack. Her right horn and the barbed nub above her nose speared the robot's side, puncturing through the hull. The beetle's tentacle coiled around her left horn and squeezed. Cracks appeared in the bony appendage, as the horn began to splinter. Until that moment, I had never heard a dinosaur shriek. It's a sound I've never forgotten.

The triceratops pushed with all her might, shoving the probe backward. Then she reared up on her hind legs, lifting the beetle off the ground. The treads spun uselessly in the air. The dinosaur shook her head savagely, and the probe slipped off her horns and crashed to the ground, landing on its roof. Saplings snapped beneath its bulk, and the ground shook. The hull crumpled, and the black smoke grew thicker.

Kasheena stretched out her hand, helping me to my feet. I winced and groaned, wiping away more blood.

"Are you injured?" she asked, her tone thick with panic. "Can you run?"

"No, but I can limp really fast. I'll be okay. Let's get out of here."

Nodding, she handed me my sword. I hadn't even realized that I'd dropped it.

"Keep up," she said, turning toward the stream. "I don't want to carry you."

Despite my injuries, I couldn't help but chuckle.

We snuck away. Kasheena had only her knife and an empty arrow quiver. I only had my knife and sword. My game bag—and the rabbits inside of it—must have slipped loose when I fell down the hill.

Behind us, the triceratops battered the smoking hulk back and forth, reducing it to nothing but twisted metal.

At last, the Chinese beetle had fallen silent.

We crossed the stream and fled through the woods, not stopping until we reached the grasslands. When we did, we collapsed on the ground, letting the sun beat down upon us. After the gloom of the forest, it felt wonderful. Kasheena cleaned my wounds as best she could, and bound the most serious cuts with leaves and grass. When she was finished, we rested for a while, holding each other close.

Eventually, we started back to the village, empty-handed but alive—and with a hunting tale to tell around the community fire.

## ACKNOWLEDGMENTS

Thanks to Jason Sizemore, Lesley Conner, and the rest of the Apex Books team, and to Paul Goblirsch and the Thunderstorm Books team. Thanks as well to my valiant pre-readers, Mark "Dezm" Sylva, Tod Clark, Stephen "Macker" McDornell, and Mike Acquavella. Thanks to Mike Lombardo, Dave Thomas, Robert Swartwood, Cathy Gonzalez, and Stephen Kozeniewski. Thanks to David J. Schow, John Skipp, Kasey Lansdale, Hal Bodner, John Urbancik, Michael Bailey, Nick Mamatas, Gene O'Neill, James A. Moore, Christopher Golden and Rio Youers. Thanks to Mary SanGiovanni. And as always, thanks to my sons.

## ALSO BY BRIAN KEENE

### THE LOST LEVEL SERIES

Hole in the World

The Lost Level

Return to the Lost Level

### THE LEVI STOLTZFUS SERIES

Dark Hollow

Ghost Walk

A Gathering of Crows

Last of the Albatwitches

Invisible Monsters

### THE EARTHWORM GODS SERIES

Earthworm Gods

Earthworm Gods II: Deluge

Earthworm Gods: Selected Scenes from the End of the World

### THE RISING SERIES

The Rising

City of the Dead

The Rising: Selected Scenes from the End of the World

The Rising: Deliverance

THE LABYRINTH SERIES

The Seven

THE CLICKERS SERIES (with J.F. Gonzalez)

Clickers II: The Next Wave

Clickers III: Dagon Rising

Clickers vs. Zombies

Clickers Forever

THE ROGAN SERIES (with Steven L. Shrewsbury)

King of the Bastards

Throne of the Bastards

NON-SERIES

Alone

An Occurrence in Crazy Bear Valley

The Cage

Castaways

The Complex

The Damned Highway (with Nick Mamatas)

Darkness on the Edge of Town

Dead Sea

Entombed

Ghoul

The Girl on the Glider

Jack's Magic Beans

Kill Whitey

Liber Nigrum Scientia Secreta (with J.F. Gonzalez)

Pressure

School's Out

Scratch

Shades (with Geoff Cooper)

Take the Long Way Home

Tequila's Sunrise

Terminal

Urban Gothic

COLLECTIONS

Blood on the Page: The Complete Short Fiction, Vol. 1

All Dark, All the Time: The Complete Short Fiction, Vol. 2

Trigger Warnings

Unsafe Spaces

Other Words

Where We Live and Die

## ABOUT THE AUTHOR

BRIAN KEENE writes novels, comic books, short fiction, and occasional journalism for money. He is the author of over fifty books, mostly in the horror, crime, and dark fantasy genres. His 2003 novel, *The Rising*, is often credited (along with Robert Kirkman's *The Walking Dead* comic and Danny Boyle's *28 Days Later* film) with inspiring pop culture's current interest in zombies. Keene's novels have been translated into German, Spanish, Polish, Italian, French, Taiwanese, and many more. In addition to his own original work, Keene has written for media properties such as *Doctor Who, The X-Files, Hellboy, Masters of the Universe*, and *Aliens*.

Several of Keene's novels have been developed for film, including *Ghoul, The Naughty List, The Ties That Bind*, and *Fast Zombies Suck*. Keene's work has been praised in such diverse places as *The New York Times, The History Channel, The Howard Stern Show, CNN.com, Publisher's Weekly, Media Bistro, Fangoria Magazine*, and *Rue Morgue Magazine*.

He has won numerous awards and honors, including the 2014 World Horror Grandmaster Award, 2016 Imadjinn Award for Best Fantasy Novel, 2001 Bram Stoker Award for Nonfiction, 2003 Bram Stoker Award for First Novel, 2004 Shocker Award for Book of the Year, and Honors from United States Army International Security Assistance Force in Afghanistan and

Whiteman A.F.B. (home of the B-2 Stealth Bomber) 509th Logistics Fuels Flight.

A prolific public speaker, Keene has delivered talks at conventions, college campuses, theaters, and inside Central Intelligence Agency headquarters in Langley, VA.

The father of two sons, Keene lives in rural Pennsylvania.

*For more information:*

www.briankeene.com

Lightning Source UK Ltd.
Milton Keynes UK
UKHW010610231119
354067UK00001B/14/P

9 781937 009632